MURDER RINGS A BELL

Rooftop Garden Cozy Mysteries, Book 4

THEA CAMBERT

Summer Prescott Books Publishing

Copyright 2020 Summer Prescott Books

All Rights Reserved. No part of this publication nor any of the information herein may be quoted from, nor reproduced, in any form, including but not limited to: printing, scanning, photocopying, or any other printed, digital, or audio formats, without prior express written consent of the copyright holder.

**This book is a work of fiction. Any similarities to persons, living or dead, places of business, or situations past or present, is completely unintentional.

CHAPTER 1

Alice Maguire stood at the edge of her rooftop garden and looked down over Main Street. It was a glorious summer morning in Blue Valley, Tennessee. Across the way, she could see Marge Hartfield opening the windows of her apartment, which was situated above her candle shop, the Waxy Wick. Marge caught sight of Alice and gave her a wave before going back inside.

Next to the Waxy Wick, Trinkets, Blue Valley's favorite souvenir and doodad shop, was still locked up tight, but Koi Butler, the yoga teacher who lived above the shop was already moving through a vinyasa flow on the rooftop garden he and Marge shared.

"Talk about hot yoga!" Owen James said. Alice's dear

friend and neighbor emerged from his apartment carrying a crisp white bag from his bakery, Sourdough, downstairs.

"I thought we were being virtuous with our run this morning," said Franny Brown, coming out of her own apartment, carrying a carafe of coffee. Franny owned Joe's, Blue Valley's favorite coffee shop. "Please tell me there are cinnamon rolls in that bag!"

"You mean *sin*-amon rolls," said Owen with a scoff.

"That's what I said."

"No, you didn't. You said cinnamon rolls."

"How can you tell the difference?"

"Oh, believe me, there's a difference." Owen opened the bag and the creamy, spicy aroma of his signature blend of ingredients wafted out. Franny set the coffee on the table next to three mugs, alongside today's issue of the *Blue Valley Post*, which Alice had brought up from her bookshop, The Paper Owl.

"He's right," said Alice, taking a whiff of the bakery bag's contents. "These are definitely *sin-amon* rolls."

"Did we run far enough this morning to burn off even

half of one of those?" asked Franny as she poured the coffee.

"Um. No." Owen placed the three gooey rolls, still hot from the oven, onto plates.

The three friends had taken up jogging back in the fall, and had been fairly good about holding each other accountable and getting out at least four times a week. They were none too fast, and spent a significant part of the "run" talking, walking, and laughing, but they covered all of Main Street, Town Park, and the downtown neighborhoods, so what they lacked in speed, they made up for in distance.

"My mom wants me to wear her wedding dress, but if I eat too many of these, I'll never be able to get into it," said Franny, taking a big bite of her roll. "I mean, the wedding's only four months away—and my mom is petite!"

"We may have to start running further," said Alice. "Owen, these are amazing, as usual."

"They are, aren't they?" Owen leaned back in his chair and closed his eyes, enjoying the sunshine.

The historic, renovated building the three of them

shared had been divided into three separate shops. Alice's bookstore, The Paper Owl, stood between Franny's coffee shop and Owen's bakery. Each shop boasted a tiny apartment above it, reachable by a beautiful old wooden staircase at the back of The Paper Owl. When Alice had moved into her apartment, she'd noticed that the roof space just outside the french doors in her bookshelf-lined living room was being wasted. It was basically an open, empty space with one folding chair set in the middle. So, she decided to create a garden, starting with a few cheerful pots of geraniums.

Once Franny and Owen joined in the effort, the rooftop had been transformed into a haven above Main Street, replete with climbing vines and potted trees, herbs, and flowers—and of course, the all-important twinkle lights that Alice tended to string everywhere she went. There was a small café table surrounded by comfortable Adirondack chairs—five of them, because they were often joined by two additional friends: Alice's brother Ben, who was a Blue Valley police officer, and Luke Evans, a police detective and the man Alice was currently dating.

When other shop owners had seen Alice's rooftop garden, many of them had followed suit, so that now,

Mainstreet was dotted with beautiful little gardens above many of its gracious old buildings.

In the spring, Franny and Ben had gotten engaged, so this summer, Alice and Owen had agreed to help them plan their wedding, which was scheduled for the fall.

"What do we have planned today?" Owen asked, taking a sip of coffee.

"Joe's is already hopping downstairs," said Franny. "The tourists have started arriving for the weekend."

"Ah, yes. The onslaught," said Owen with a smile. "The smart ones always come in on Thursdays, to beat the crowds. And, frankly, I think weekends should always start on Thursdays, don't you?"

Every July, the town held its Annual Independence Day Weekend Celebration at Blue Lake, which lay only half a mile from Main Street. The cozy town of Blue Valley, snuggled up against Tennessee's Smoky Mountains, had grown up around the lake, which was fed every spring by the melting snow that ran down the mountainsides. Blue Valley was just far enough off the beaten path that the tourists who came there were the type who were willing to wind a little further back into the mountains—but they always managed to find it, and returned season after season for the town's many festivals and fairs.

"Is Beth working down at Joe's this morning?" asked Alice.

"Yep," said Franny. "She's putting in extra hours through the weekend."

"Hilda, too," said Owen, whose assistant at Sourdough, Hilda Becker, hated festivals and crowds, but could bake up a storm. "She actually *likes* to work extra when there's an influx of tourists, just to avoid going out."

"Is Lacie home for the summer?" Franny asked.

Lacie Blake's parents, Doug and Barb, owned Sugarbuzz, the town's gourmet chocolate shop, just a few doors down. But, Lacie had been helping Alice out in the bookshop for years, and still did, whenever she was home from college.

"Yep," said Alice with a contented sigh. "She's more than happy to help out in the shop this summer."

"College kids can always use a little extra cash," said Owen.

"The weekend's going to be even busier than usual with that doctors' conference in town," said Franny. "I love doctors. They drink a ton of coffee."

"They also eat a lot of sweets," said Owen. "Cha-ching! Oh—I'm starting to explore ideas for your wedding cake, Franny. I'll start plying you both with samples tonight."

"This is the best day ever," Alice observed. "We're having sin-amon rolls for breakfast and cake for dinner."

"So . . . Tell us," Franny said, grinning widely at Alice. "How was your date with Detective Hot-Stuff last night?"

"Oh yes, spill!" said Owen, leaning forward in his chair. "We want all the details."

Making an effort to keep her tone light, Alice said, "Luke cancelled at the last minute."

"What?" said Franny. "Why?"

"He said he had a terrible headache," said Alice, shrugging one shoulder.

"That old excuse," said Owen, rolling his eyes.

"Owen!" Franny slapped him on the arm. "I'm sure he really just . . . had a headache."

Alice shifted in her chair and looked out over Main Street. "It still sort of sometimes bothers me that Luke was engaged before," she admitted.

"*'Still sort of sometimes*?'" Owen shook his head. "Please, Alice. We can see right through your flimsy façade. You've been stewing, haven't you?"

He looked at Franny, who nodded in agreement. "Yep, she's stewing," Franny said. "Do you know anything about Luke's ex?"

"I know *she* was the one who broke it off," said Alice. "That's what bugs me the most. I mean, I guess they'd still be together if it had been up to Luke."

"And, then, he never would've come to Blue Valley, and he never would've met you, and he *definitely* would've ended up divorced and unhappy, wondering how he could've mistaken the woman he married for the love of his life, who was still out there somewhere, and quite possibly now married to someone else." Owen coughed a little. "Wow, that was a long sentence. Even for me."

"What if she was, like, a rocket scientist or super model or something?" asked Alice.

"Stew, stew, stew," said Owen shaking his head at Alice.

"The thing to remember is, Luke's with you, now," Franny said cheerfully.

"And, anyone can see he's totally smitten," added Owen.

"You're right, of course," Alice admitted. "I'm being silly. I am, after all, a successful businesswoman—"

"With excellent friends," said Owen.

"And red hair," said Franny. "I bet Miss Rocket-Super Model doesn't have gorgeous red hair like you."

"Thanks, guys," said Alice. "I feel better, now. Luke probably just had a really bad headache. End of story."

"Is that why he's so grumpy?" Ben Maguire emerged from Alice's apartment. Her cat, Poppy, immediately jumped up from where she'd been taking a sunshine nap and ran to entwine herself around Ben's ankles, almost tripping him. "Alice, this cat is going to kill me someday."

"She loves her Uncle Ben! How can you be so cold?"

Ben gave Franny a kiss on the top of her head and sat down in the chair next to her, allowing Poppy to jump up into his lap.

"So, Luke's been acting grumpy at the station?" Alice asked, still working to keep her tone casual.

"Saw him there this morning before I headed out," said Ben, nodding. "He didn't seem himself at all. He actually yelled at Dewey."

"Officer Dewey?" Franny asked, surprised. "How could anyone yell at that sweet little guy?"

"Well, to be fair, Dewey let a couple of squirrels loose in the station, so—"

"Squirrels? Are you kidding?" asked Alice with a laugh.

"Doc and Mrs. Howard had a nest of them in their attic, so Dewey went over and lured them into a Havahart trap using birdseed. He stopped off at the station before heading out to the woods to set them free." Ben shook his head at the memory. "Then, Dewey stumbled, and the squirrels flew through the air, and . . . Anyway, Luke was clearly on edge."

Alice frowned and walked over to the building's façade that enclosed the rooftop garden. She looked down at Main Street, where shops were beginning to open and people were stopping in here and there.

"Ah-ha!" said Owen, getting up and joining Alice. He nudged her with his elbow. "Still stewing, are we?"

"That, or she's wondering what ever happened to the squirrels," said Franny.

"Alice, we have more important things to think about than displaced squirrels," said Ben. "We've only got two more days until Saturday's big race, and we have to be ready."

For Ben and Alice, the highlight of the holiday weekend was always the Blue Lake Independence Day Pedal Boat Regatta. They'd won it seven years in a row, but the competition was mounting. The winners got to keep the coveted Champion's Cup for a year. In fact, the first case Ben had solved as a green police officer was when the cup had gone missing twelve years earlier. He'd finally discovered that Old

Lottie Ferguson had it. Old Lottie owned the local nursery, The Green Thumb, and had accidentally planted a trailing vine in the cup after winning that year's regatta, and then had forgotten all about it. In time, the vine had grown, completely obscuring the cup. Thinking it had been stolen, Lottie had called in the police—and was all too happy to replant the vine and sweep the whole incident under the rug once the case had been solved. Now, the Champion's Cup spent half the year on Alice's bookshelf, and the other half on Ben's fireplace mantle.

"I'll meet you here at the bookstore after work, okay?" Alice asked.

"Good. I get off at five. We've got to work on strategy. We need to perfect our turns and our launch. Have you been keeping up with your squats?"

"Yep. Franny and Owen have been doing them with me."

"And, we just did our three-mile run," Franny added.

"Excellent," said Ben, standing to go and catching a glimpse of sugary glaze on their plates. "Easy on the sin-amon rolls, Alice. You have to train like an athlete. That means healthy food. I'm off to work. Hopefully, the rest of the day will be squirrel-free."

"I personally love squirrels," said Franny.

"I've got nothing against them," said Ben. "But, they don't belong in people's attics—or in the police station." He gave Poppy a farewell pat on the head, lightly kissed Franny on the cheek, and was off.

"Gosh, I love that man," said Franny, watching him go. "He's so cute in his uniform."

"We have a lot of planning to do before your wedding in October," said Alice. "The gown, the flowers, the church, the guestlist . . ."

"But first, cake," said Owen, standing. "I'm off to work. See you both tonight!"

CHAPTER 2

Marge Hartfield had just dropped off a case of her special Fourth of July candles, including *Pie Eating Contest*, which smelled like cherries and pastry crust, and *Uncle Sam's Choice*, which was red, white, and blue, and somehow smelled exactly like a summer day at the lake. Then, there was the very interesting *Fireworks!* candle, which smelled a bit like a spent bottle rocket or sparkler. Alice wasn't wild about those, but they sold like hotcakes every year, so she always stocked them in the bookshop.

The last few customers of the day were still browsing the shelves as Alice turned over the closed sign on the front door, telling the dawdlers to take all the time they needed. Meanwhile, she got busy arranging the new candles in The Paper Owl's candle corner. Franny walked over from Joe's through the wide cased opening that separated the coffee shop from the bookstore. Alice and Franny had always found that their customers liked wandering between the two shops, since books and coffee paired so well.

"Good day?" Franny asked, then stopped abruptly and sniffed the air. "Oh, good heavens. Is that Marge's stinky *Fireworks!* candle I smell?"

"You guessed it," said Alice, who was not at all surprised that Franny had nailed the candle by its scent. Franny had an extremely keen sense of smell.

"Who buys those?" Franny pinched her nose shut. "They smell like rotten eggs and smoke mixed together."

"Sulfur," said Alice.

"What?"

"Sulfur. It's in the black powder they use in fireworks."

"Well, Marge has captured that smell perfectly. Just don't light any of those up, okay?"

"Not a chance," Alice said, chuckling. "So, how was your day?"

"Very busy," said Franny. "Just closed up shop. You?"

"Tons of sales with the tourists in for the long weekend. It was a much better day than yesterday, I'm happy to say."

"Why? What happened yesterday?"

"Nothing major. Just this one rude customer. I get one every now and then, but she really ticked me off. Today was smooth sailing, though."

A young woman approached the counter with a copy of Agatha Christie's *And Then There Were None*. Alice was immediately struck by her sunflower blond hair and bright green eyes. "I heard her—the rude customer?" the woman said in a high, sing-songy voice, taking out a twenty-dollar bill. "I was in here yesterday when she came in. I don't blame you for being ticked off." She glanced down, looking a little embarrassed. "Sorry. Didn't mean to eavesdrop."

"Not at all!" said Alice, ringing up the book. "I'm glad I'm not the only one who thought she was crass."

"Oh, she was worse than crass," said the woman. "I don't understand people like that."

"Wow. What did she do?" asked Franny.

Alice gave a little sigh. "Well, first, she walked in and looked at the shop like it was a hovel. She said the selection of books was pitiful. She was on the hunt for a book I didn't have. When I offered to order it for her, she got frustrated and said not to bother. She left in a huff."

"That's right," said the customer. "She talked so loudly, I heard the whole thing. Sometimes doctors can be a little bit full of themselves."

"How did you know she was a doctor?" asked Franny.

"I just assumed, because she was wearing one of those lanyards they're all wearing—with that medical conference or whatever it is in town?"

"I assumed so, too," said Alice, handing the customer her book in a tote bag with The Paper Owl's logo on the front. "There are tons of them here for the weekend."

The woman nodded. "I found out all about the conference when we got to town and tried to get a room at the Valley Inn. It's booked solid with doctors."

"You know what bugged me most about that woman? She seemed to be sizing me up. I know that sounds crazy, but she kept looking me up and down and sneering." Alice scoffed. "I probably just imagined that. I'm being silly."

"No, you're not," said Franny. "Hopefully, she was a one-time customer."

"Oh, I doubt she'd want to come back to this shop," said Alice. "You could've cut the disdain with a knife."

"Well, I think you handled the situation very well," said the customer, smiling over her shoulder as she opened the door and headed back out to Main Street.

"Thank you!" Alice called after her.

"She was nice," said Franny.

"Thank goodness most customers are."

The bells on the front door jingled again as Ben came in. He held the door for Alice's last few customers—in this case, a couple with a baby strapped to the dad's belly. Ben smiled at the little family as they left the shop, and Alice knew exactly what her brother was thinking when he turned his gaze to Franny.

"That could be you two someday," Alice said with a grin.

Franny giggled. "We have to get married first."

"We're in our thirties now." Alice wiggled her eyebrows at Franny. "Don't wait too long."

"You should talk!" said Franny.

Franny and Alice were both thirty and had been friends since the tender age of twelve, when Franny's family moved to Blue Valley. Alice had been relieved to find a kindred spirit in the midst of middle school, and they'd been inseparable ever since. Owen, also thirty, had arrived in town six years ago, fresh out of culinary school in Nashville, and his amazing breads, cookies, and pastries had set him on the fast track to becoming a beloved citizen of Blue Valley.

"*What* should Alice talk about? Fill me in." Owen had just walked through the door at the back of The Paper Owl. The door—fashioned to look like just another bookshelf —led to the hallway that housed the staircase to their apartments. The hallway itself ran behind all three shops, and Alice had been beside herself with excitement when she'd recently had her door remodeled to be a functioning bookshelf.

"The fact that the clock is ticking just as much for her as it is for me," said Franny.

"The clock? Oh! You mean, The Clock," said Owen, nodding in understanding. "I don't have a clock myself, but I'm definitely looking forward to spoiling all your children someday."

"Okay, enough talk about babies," Alice said.

"Good. Don't you two have someplace to be? I mean, some training to do? That regatta's not going to win itself, now is it?" said Owen.

"He's right, Alice," said Ben. "We've only got today and tomorrow. We need to get over to the lake."

"I'll go change," said Alice, jogging to the back of the shop.

"Good!" Ben called after her. "Because *Maguires' Magnificent Maelstrom Vortex* waits for no one!"

"Who came up with that name for your boat,

anyway?" Owen hopped up to sit on the counter and crossed his ankles. "I mean, aren't a maelstrom and a vortex basically the same thing?"

"Yes," Alice said, opening the bookcase door. "But, we don't care."

"That's right," said Ben. "The other boats better watch out for a storm when we blow them all out of the water Saturday morning."

"Pretty sure you'll win again this year?" asked Owen.

"Are you kidding? We've got the boat. The maneuvers. The tenacity. We've won seven years running," said Ben. "It's in the bag,"

"We're not letting go of the Champion's Cup for anything," said Alice, giving her brother an air high-five.

CHAPTER 3

"We'll decorate the *Maelstrom* tomorrow night," said Ben, snapping the buckles of his lifejacket.

"Get her all ship-shape?" asked Alice with a giggle, as she pulled the tarp off the boat.

"Very funny."

They were standing on Ben's dock, just in front of his little house. The pedal boat, which was bobbing up and down with the choppy waves the breeze was sending across the water's surface, was shiny and black, and bore the words *Maelstrom Vortex* in gold letters across the back, along with a picture of a wicked-looking horned Viking helmet.

"Little north wind tonight. That's good," said Ben. "Training in the wind will give us a competitive edge."

"I hope we have some real competition this year," said Alice. "It's boring to win the regatta with too much of a lead."

Ben and Alice each unhooked one of the carabiners from the two metal rings attached to the dock for the purpose of mooring a pedal boat. They'd been pedaling boats across Blue Lake since childhood, when the family would come out to spend summer Saturdays swimming and picnicking. Alice would never forget the year their dad, Martin Maguire, had taken them out for their first boat ride from the little marina on the lake next to the town dock. The marina, truth be told, was more of a fishing shack, stocked with plenty of bamboo poles and hooks and home to a fleet of a dozen well-maintained pedal boats that were brought into the water every summer and packed safely away every winter.

Ben had decided way back when they were kids that he would someday have his own place on the lake and had never wavered in his resolve to find just the right spot along the shoreline. Alice loved it that Luke had also purchased a cabin just a short distance from Ben's house, and that she could walk between the two houses via a path that wound through the trees. It made her even happier that Ben and Luke were not only colleagues at the police station, but good friends as well.

"Okay, ready to launch?" Ben asked, stepping into the boat.

"Yep," said Alice, following her brother aboard. As she took her seat, Alice noticed a small movement down the shoreline, toward the town dock. "Hold it. What's that?" She reached out to still Ben's legs mid-pedal.

"What's what?" asked Ben, looking in the direction of Alice's focus. "Oh. I see it. Not sure . . ."

"I think it might be a dog," said Alice. "But, it's not moving at all. Is it a statue of a dog?"

"A statue of a dog at the edge of the lake?" Ben said. "Right, Alice." He let out a little snort and shook his head.

"It is dog-shaped," Alice insisted. "Let's pedal over."

"Fine," said Ben. "I can tell, you won't be able to focus until we do."

They pedaled out into the water, hung a sharp left, and followed the arc of the shoreline toward the town dock. Soon, the dog statue came into clearer view—except that it wasn't a statue at all.

"He just wagged his tail!" said Alice. "It's a real dog!"

"What's he doing out here all alone?" asked Ben, turning the rudder to steer them to shore.

The little black and white border collie gave Ben and Alice a quick wag of his tail as they dragged the pedal boat up onto the shore, then returned his gaze to the water.

"Poor little guy," said Alice, reaching out a tentative hand to stroke the dog's silky head. "Where's your family?"

She looked out at the water, but there wasn't another boat in sight, and the little dog refused to take his eyes off the lake. He did give Alice a grateful lick when she tried to comfort him.

"Sure hope his owner's not out swimming in this

wind," said Ben, scanning the lake.

"Can we take him home?" asked Alice. "We can't leave him here all alone."

"Why don't we go ahead and practice, give his family a chance to come back, and then when we're done, if he's still here, we'll take him to my house. I'll make a few calls to try to find his owner."

"Okay," said Alice, giving the dog one last pat on the head. "Now, don't be afraid. We'll be right back," she assured him.

But, when she and Ben got back into the boat, they were surprised that the little dog jumped in after them. He seemed intent upon ensconcing himself on the deck that ran along the stern end of the boat. He sat up straight on full alert, like a furry ship's captain.

"Well, the extra weight will add resistance," Ben reasoned as they backed out into the water and turned about.

They picked up speed, pedaling out toward the center of the lake, when the dog jumped up suddenly and began barking. It was then that Alice noticed his green collar had a silver tag dangling from it that had been tucked into his long hair. She squinted into the setting sunlight, straining to read the tag.

"Finn! His name is Finn!" said Alice.

"Hey, Finn, what's wrong, boy?" asked Ben, who'd stopped pedaling and turned around in his seat to pet the agitated dog.

Suddenly, Finn leapt into the water and began swimming further out toward the center of the lake.

"Hit it, Alice!" Ben said, and they sped off after the dog. They soon caught up and pulled Finn safely back into the boat. Ben opened a small storage compartment between the seats and pulled out a towel, which Alice wrapped around Finn.

"What on earth?" Alice scanned the water's surface in the direction Finn had been so determined to go. "Oh, my gosh, Ben. What's that?"

Ben looked where Alice was pointing.

"I don't know. It looks like—" He stopped short and swallowed.

"It looks like a body," said Alice.

CHAPTER 4

It took them some time and a great deal of effort, but within half an hour, Alice and Ben had managed to drag the body of a woman aboard the *Maelstrom* while avoiding toppling over into the water themselves or losing hold of Finn.

"This is heartbreaking," said Alice sadly. "This must be Finn's owner."

Finn, apparently satisfied that his work was done, sat close to Alice, quietly looking at the motionless form of the drowned woman who lay face-down across the back deck of the boat.

"You brought your cell, didn't you? Give Luke a call. Tell him to meet us on the shore."

Alice quickly made the call, shakily telling Luke what had happened, and then she and Ben pedaled furiously to shore—which wasn't hard with the wind now at their backs.

Alice felt a wave of relief when she saw Luke in the distance, running over from the direction of his cabin. The moment they brushed the shoreline, Ben stood and climbed over the front of the boat, jumping down into calf-deep water to pull it ashore.

Alice waved at Luke, who was getting closer. "Luke!" she called. "Thank goodness!"

"What's going on?" he called back.

At the sound of Luke's voice, Finn instantly jumped up and leaped over the front of the boat, landing nimbly on the pebbled ground, and took off running until he met Luke with a wagging tail and soft whimpering noises.

Luke looked momentarily stunned, then bent down to hug the dog.

"Finn!" he said. "What are you doing here?"

Alice climbed out of the boat, and Finn ran excitedly

between her and Luke, as if introducing them to one another.

"You know this little guy?" asked Alice.

"We've got a body. Looks like a drowning victim," said Ben, pulling the boat even further onto the shore and going around the side to carefully carry the dead woman to a grassy area where he laid her down.

Alice saw the woman's face for the first time and gasped. "I know her! I mean, I've seen her before. She was in my shop yesterday."

"Really?" asked Ben. "Do you know her name? Did she buy anything?"

Alice suddenly felt dizzy and braced herself against Ben's side. "She was . . . She was very rude, actually." She looked at Luke and saw that he'd turned as white as a ghost. "Wait a minute," she said slowly. "How do you know this dog?"

"This is . . ." Luke looked sadly at the dead woman, then at Alice. "This is Alexandra Darlington. She's an ER doctor at Tennessee General Hospital. In Nashville."

"You knew her?" asked Alice, her heart in her throat.

"She's . . . She was my ex-fiancé. And this," he looked down at Finn, who sat obediently at his feet. "This is Finn. He was our dog."

CHAPTER 5

Alice had never been so glad to walk out onto her rooftop garden. She flicked a switch and hundreds of twinkle lights came on, illuminating the dusky evening and all of the many plants. It was unseasonably cool for a Tennessee summer night. Alice considered anything below sixty-five degrees downright chilly this time of year—but, to be fair, she required a light sweater even at seventy-five degrees.

"This calls for cake," said Owen, who emerged from his apartment with a sympathetic look on his face.

"You heard?" asked Alice.

"I told him. Ben called," said Franny, coming out of her own apartment with three steaming mugs. "I'm so sorry, Alice." Franny set the mugs down on the café table.

Alice was pleasantly surprised when she took a sip and realized the drink was hot chocolate—Franny's special recipe, which was swirled with marshmallow cream.

Owen set a bakery box from Sourdough on the table as well. "Wedding cake ideas," he said, opening the box to reveal a dozen tiny cakes—three each of four different varieties.

"Oh, I need that," said Alice, taking a deep breath and savoring the smells of frosting and freshly baked, moist cake.

"But first tell us all about it," said Owen. "What happened out at the lake?"

Alice told them about meeting Finn on the shore and pedaling out, and the shock of finding Alexandra Darlington's body.

Franny laid a hand on Alice's arm. "How are you feeling about . . . all of this?"

"Confused," said Alice. "I don't know what to think. I'm torn between feeling oddly insecure, knowing that Luke's ex was a beautiful ER doctor, feeing horrified that she drowned right here in Blue Valley, *and* feeling upset that Luke cancelled our date Wednesday night—and has been acting strangely. I mean, did he cancel on me to see her?" Alice sighed. "It's not as though I can logically be jealous of a dead woman. And, I know it's petty to even have these thoughts. I just . . . feel rattled by this whole thing."

"Understandable," said Owen. "But, Luke is a good guy. Anyone who's ever seen the way he looks at you knows he's crazy about you."

"No doubt," Franny agreed.

"He talked to Ben and me tonight, while we were waiting for the ambulance. About how he first fell in love with Alexandra—how she'd seemed funny and smart and kind. They met during her residency at Tennessee General."

Alice told them how Luke had said that Alexandra—or Allie, as he'd called her—had graduated at the top of her class and been awarded a prestigious post at the best hospital in the state. How she'd changed over time, to be more concerned with her career and getting ahead than with her relationships. He'd said he wasn't even sure when she'd stopped loving him—that he sort of just got lost in the shuffle of it all.

"I guess time will tell how this all pans out," said Alice, slumping into her chair.

"In the meantime," said Owen. "Take a bite of this."

He handed out the first cake sample. "This is a vanilla cake with pecan praline buttercream frosting and a dark chocolate ganache filling."

"Oh, my gosh." Franny moaned in pleasure. "That is amazing."

"Owen, this is fantastic." Alice licked a stray glob of frosting off her finger.

"This is the one," said Franny, taking another bite. "It's perfect."

"No, it isn't," said Owen, scrutinizing his own bite. "I'm not quite happy with it. Let's try this one." He took out the next set of mini-cakes.

"Wow! Oh, *this* is it!" said Franny, closing her eyes as she chewed.

"This is an almond cake with salted caramel-laced buttercream, topped with a layer of caramel-amaretto fondant," said Owen, thoughtfully tasting the cake.

"I love this one," said Alice.

"Nope, this isn't the one," said Owen. He passed around a third sample. "Raspberry-filled white chocolate topped with milk chocolate macarons."

Alice bit into the crisp macaron on the top of her little cake. Her eyes widened. "It's fabulous, Owen! I mean, I would get married *just* to have this cake!"

"Try this one," Owen said, taking out the fourth and final sample of the evening. "It's a pink champagne cake, layered with fresh strawberries, and covered in vanilla bean buttercream."

"Owen, I can't decide!" said Franny. "These are amazing. I love them all!"

"Oh, I know they're amazing," Owen said with a frown. "But, these aren't . . . *Franny* enough. I'll keep working on it."

"Well, if you want to keep baking cakes, I'll be glad to keep tasting them," said Alice, taking a sip of hot chocolate and snuggling back into her chair. "And, you were right: I do feel a little better now."

"Alice!" a voice from below the garden called.

"Who—" Owen jumped up and peered over the building's twinkle light-lined façade. "It's Luke. He's standing down on Main Street."

Alice hurried to Owen's side and peeked down. "Luke? What are you doing down there?"

"Wherefore art thou, Luke?" Owen called in his best and most dramatic British accent. "Deny the father and refuse—"

"Can it, Owen," said Alice.

"I tried to call your cell phone, but you didn't answer," Luke said. "Can I come up?"

"Go ahead, Rapunzel. Let down your hair," said Owen with a smirk. Then he whispered, "Told you he's crazy about you."

"You're getting your epic romances mixed up," said Alice, raising an eyebrow at Owen. "Stay right there, Luke! I'll come unlock the door." Alice jogged into her apartment.

Usually when Luke came, he was either with Ben, who had a key to the front door of The Paper Owl, or

Alice was expecting him, so she'd unlocked the door in advance of his arrival. A few moments later, Alice returned to the garden with Luke in tow.

"Sorry, we ate all the cake," said Franny.

"Cake?" asked Luke, taking a seat.

"Wedding cake," said Alice.

Poppy, who was almost as enamored with Luke as she was with Ben, came trotting over and jumped into his lap. He mechanically scratched her behind the ears, and she sniffed his hand suspiciously.

"She can smell Finn," said Alice, watching Luke's face carefully, trying to read his emotional state—not an easy feat with a man who generally guarded his feelings.

"Ah," said Luke, nodding numbly.

"You look spent," said Owen. "Sorry about your, um, friend."

"Alexandra was no friend of mine," Luke answered, looking straight at Alice. "She was a manipulative, arrogant, passive-aggressive woman who ditched me and stole my dog."

"So, how's Finn doing?" Alice asked quietly.

Luke let out a long sigh. "He's doing much better, now. He's at the cabin. I hate that Alexandra drowned, but I'm awfully glad to have Finn back. That's probably a horrible thing to say."

"No, it isn't," said Alice, feeling her heart warm to Luke a bit.

"We should probably leave you two alone," said Owen, giving Franny a not-so-subtle wink and a nudge.

"No!" Luke said so suddenly that Alice jumped. "I need your help."

CHAPTER 6

Owen and Franny, who'd been about to retreat, settled back into their chairs.

"If you need our help, you've got it," said Alice, noticing Luke's shoulders tensed up to near his ears and a furrow between his eyebrows. She'd never seen him truly ruffled and had come to expect his calm demeanor to be unshakeable. Now, she wasn't so sure.

"I can't believe I'm doing this," Luke muttered. "For obvious reasons, I'm not part of the investigation into Alexandra's death."

"That makes sense," said Owen. "But, what is there to investigate? She drowned, right?"

"I wish it was that simple," said Luke. "Old Zeb Clark, the coroner, suspects Alexandra didn't drown at all, and he's passed her case on to the medical examiner." Luke rubbed his temples. "Seems Alexandra was dead before she ever hit the water."

"What killed her, then?" asked Alice.

"Some kind of very strong impact."

"Like what?"

"I can't believe I'm talking about this." Luke looked apologetically at each of them. "Ben's still on the investigation, and he'll get to the bottom of it. I know he will. It's just that . . ." Alice noticed a little falter in Luke's voice. "You've helped us out on cases before," he said, finally. "If you should have any ideas, or find any clues . . ."

"Of course, we'll tell you. And Ben," said Alice.

"Are you saying Alexandra's death was no accident? She was murdered?" asked Franny.

Luke nodded solemnly, his eyes coming to rest on Alice.

"When did she get into town?" Alice asked quietly.

"Late Tuesday."

"Did you know she was coming?"

"Absolutely not."

"Had you seen her since her arrival?"

Luke paused, his eyes full of regret. "Yes."

"Wednesday." It came out as more a statement than a question. Alice felt a lump forming in her throat. "When you had that headache?"

"That part was true," said Luke, reaching out to touch Alice's hand. "Alexandra showed up at my cabin Wednesday morning."

"Why?"

"She wanted to talk."

"About?"

Luke paused. "About us."

"She wanted you back." Alice slid her hand away from Luke's.

"She brought Finn over. She was crying. Said she'd made the biggest mistake of her life. Asked for another chance." Luke dropped his head into his hands.

"What did you do?" asked Franny, scooting her chair a little closer to Alice's and putting a loyal arm around her friend.

"I asked her to give Finn back. I love that dog," said Luke.

"Was that it?" asked Owen, scooting his chair a little closer to Alice on the other side.

"That was it. I told Allie—or Alexandra, I should say." He looked thoughtful, as if calling to mind a faraway memory. "She hated being called Allie. It was her nickname during med school. But, she changed so much over time . . . Anyway, I told her I'd made a fresh start here, that I'd had time to think about what happened between us. That I didn't want to see her again. Ever." He looked at Alice and paused. "And, that I deeply care for someone I've met here."

Alice felt tears stinging her eyes.

"Did you tell her who I am?"

"No."

"Well, she must've asked around, because she came into my bookshop later that day and was horrible to me."

"*She* was the rude customer?" asked Franny. "The one who was sizing you up? Of course! It all makes sense now!"

"She sized you up?" asked Luke.

"Checking out the competition, was she?" said Owen.

"Thought I was imagining it," said Alice.

"Blue Valley's a very small town," said Owen. "She could've asked any local and found out who Luke Evans is dating."

"Who would want Alexandra dead?" asked Alice.

"That's my problem," said Luke. "Who did she know here other than me? Zeb says time of death was late Wednesday night. I'd seen her Wednesday. We'd argued. Then, I had to go and cancel the only plans I had that night, so I have no alibi. I'm the prime suspect at this point."

"Steady, now," said Owen, who'd noticed that Alice's face had turned bright red.

Alice took a deep, calming breath. "You said Alexandra was an ER doctor," she said. "Was she in town for the doctors' conference?"

"Yes," said Luke. "That was her excuse for coming here, anyway."

"Well, then, she probably knew someone here other than you. Not a local, maybe. But, one of the other doctors. Surely she knew at least one or two of them."

"You're probably right. They're here from all over the region," said Luke.

"It's a good place to start our investigation," said Alice. "We look for connections with the other doctors. Maybe we'll come across someone who had some kind of beef with Alexandra. Was she staying at the Valley Inn?"

"Yes," said Luke, standing and placing Poppy gently on the ground. "I'd better be going," he said apologetically. "I left Finn alone at the cabin, and he's probably starting to get antsy." He let out a long exhale. "I feel terrible talking about all of this. I just want to get to the bottom of it and move on with my life. You three have proved you have superior deductive reasoning skills and sharp instincts."

"Well," said Owen, smiling modestly, "we can't help it that we're brilliant."

"We'll start asking around tomorrow," said Alice. She grabbed Luke's arm and gave it a squeeze. "We're on the case. I'll walk you out."

CHAPTER 7

Alice's alarm clock landed with a thud on the floor next to her nightstand. She hadn't meant to whack it quite so hard when it rang after a third round of snoozing. She wouldn't have believed it was time to get up were it not for the light coming through the windows and the sounds of birds singing cheerfully out in the rooftop garden. Confounded birds!

And then there was Poppy, who had roused herself out of the cozy nest she'd made in the bed, and padded over to sit and stare at her owner, occasionally swatting at her face with a gentle paw. This was Poppy's way of prompting Alice to get up and pour her a bowl of cat food.

Alice threw off the covers, got up, replaced the alarm

clock on the nightstand, and opened the curtains. Her large bedroom windows looked out onto the rooftop garden, and she could see that Franny and Owen were already seated and drinking coffee.

In the bathroom, Alice gathered her red curls—which were sticking out in every direction after her short but fitful sleep—into a loose knot and splashed cool water on her face. She swiped a little tinted moisturizer under her eyes to downplay the puffy shadows that stood out against her pale skin and added a swipe of peachy lipstick. Any southern woman worth her salt knew that lipstick was the difference between looking pulled together and looking haggard. Alice's mother had taught her that. After pulling on her most comfortable sleeveless summer dress and stepping into a pair of Keds, Alice went out into the garden, feeling slightly more awake.

"Coffee," she said, looking fondly at the Joe's carafe that Franny had brought up. "Oh, thank you that there is coffee in this world!"

"Good morning," said Franny, pouring Alice a cup.

"Sleeping in this morning, are we?" asked Owen, peering over the rim of his mug as he took a swallow.

"I stayed up way too late after our visit from Luke," said Alice, sitting down in her chair and wrapping her hands around the warmth of her mug.

Owen set a sweet, flaky German pretzel—one of Sourdough's specialties—on a plate in front of Alice.

"My favorite." Alice broke off a crisp piece of the pretzel and took a bite, savoring the finely chopped pecans and vanilla glaze.

"You always say everything is your favorite," said Owen with a snicker. "Now, tell us about this all-nighter of yours."

"I decided to search around online for Alexandra Darlington, MD. And, I found her," said Alice through a mouthful of the puffed pastry. "Boy, did I ever find her." Alice accidentally blew a few crumbs across the table when she spoke.

"And?"

"She had a blog. *Alexandra's Adventures*. The woman shared everything from her outfit of the day to her medical advice for head injuries."

"Seriously?" Franny's eyes widened. "Did she tell her

fans she was coming to Blue Valley for the weekend, by chance?"

"Oh, yeah," said Alice, rubbing her eyes. "She said she was off to a doctors' conference. Mentioned she was planning to set off some fireworks of her own with a special someone—"

"She was talking about Luke, no doubt," said Owen.

"Probably," said Alice, stuffing a big chunk of pretzel into her mouth.

"Did she mention where she was staying?" asked Franny.

"Yep. She even included a link to the Valley Inn's website," Alice said. "Anyone could've known Alexandra was here for the weekend, and exactly where to find her."

"If someone wanted to do away with her, it makes good sense to do the deed here," said Owen. "That way, the killer isn't tied to the location."

"Which is what makes Luke such a viable suspect when you look at the situation objectively," said Alice. "He's the only local who knew Alexandra, and their past together was rocky."

"*And,* she went to visit Luke the day she died," added Franny.

"*And,* she stole Luke's dog," said Owen.

Alice took another big bite of her pretzel, then looked at the plate and was surprised to see she'd eaten the whole pastry.

"Let's remind ourselves that we know Luke didn't do it," said Owen. "We need to formulate a plan."

"Beginning with the doctors, right?" Franny asked.

"At the Valley Inn," said Alice. "Do you both have help for this afternoon?"

"Yep, Hilda's coming in at noon," said Owen.

"Beth's working full days through the whole weekend, with all the extra customers in town," said Franny.

"Good. I've got Lacie coming at lunchtime, too. Let's meet then and go over to the Valley Inn and ask the Berkleys about Alexandra—who they saw her with, what her comings and goings were. I'm betting Luke is not the only person in town who was acquainted with the adventurous Alexandra."

CHAPTER 8

"Oh, yeah, I remember her all right." Samuel Berkley, who owned the Valley Inn with his wife, Eve, rested his elbows on the front desk. "She got in, let's see . . ." He stood upright and flipped back a page in the large guestbook that sat in the center of the tidy surface, alongside a cheerful vase of verbena. "Says here, Tuesday night at nine-thirty. That's when Ms. Darlington signed in. Eve and I were up late that night because the doctors came in from all over. I think the last few had trickled in by eleven."

"Did you see Dr. Darlington again during her stay here?" asked Alice. "Maybe going out or coming in?"

"Oh, yes, she came and went a lot. All of them do. They're having their main conference in the reception hall. They meet in there several times each day. And then in between, they wander the grounds or drive into town. The police are due here any minute, you know. They want to have a look at the lady's room. Terrible, what happened."

"It sure is," said Alice, who had a sinking feeling that Samuel didn't have much information to share. "Did Dr. Darlington seem to be spending time with any of the other doctors in particular? I mean, that you noticed?"

"Nope. But, she must have had a friend in town," said Samuel, a thoughtful expression on his face.

"Really? What makes you think that?" asked Owen, stepping closer to the desk.

"She got a note. No stamp on it, and it was left right here." He tapped the desk twice with his finger. "I figure it had to be someone local that left it. Or, I guess it could've been someone else who was staying at the inn. Hey—maybe it was your Luke Evans, Alice! She knew him. Even asked me where he lives."

Alice paled at the mention of Luke's name.

"Yep, then later, she asked me who Luke dates. Hope

it was okay with you that I told her. Everyone in town knows, after all. You two sure make a handsome couple."

"Could we see her room?" Franny blurted out, saving the flustered Alice from responding.

"You all trying to solve the mystery?" Samuel glanced around and lowered his voice. "You know, I'm something of an amateur sleuth myself."

"Are you?" asked Alice.

"I thought so," said Owen. "I could tell by the way you deduced that the note was sent locally."

Samuel looked pleased at this remark.

"Let's go. You can see the room before the police arrive, as long as no one touches anything," said Samuel, grabbing a keyring with about a hundred keys jingling on it.

"Never hurts to ask," Franny whispered as they followed Samuel from the reception area, through a cozy dining room with a fireplace, and out of the main inn house. Outside, a large garden was scattered with chairs, several horseshoe courts, and a large stone fire ring surrounded by benches and baskets of firewood. Several two-story buildings, designed to look like stone cottages, were set out among the trees and connected by little stone pathways that all led back to the main inn house—a gracious old traditional place with wide porches and window boxes brimming with daisies, all surrounded by a picket fence.

"Dr. Darlington was in cottage three," said Samuel, trotting along one of the paths.

Alice smiled at the way the cottages all had different names—like *Honeysuckle Cottage*, *Shady Nook*, and cottage number three, which was called *Cobblestone Way*. Each was designed to look fairly small, but once inside, the space opened up and there were a surprising number of rooms along the hallway.

"Let's see, it'll be fourth on the left, up ahead," said Samuel, taking out a keyring.

He unlocked the door, and they all entered reverently.

"So, this was her room," Alice whispered, looking around.

"She had good taste in shoes," Owen said, pointing to the closet, where no fewer than eight pairs of shoes were neatly arranged in a row.

"All those shoes for a *weekend*?" said Franny. "So much for travelling light."

"There's the note I was telling you about," said Samuel, walking over to the desk and bending down to pull a white envelope out of the trashcan.

Dr. Alexandra Darlington was written in swirly red letters on the front, and Alice was relieved to see that it wasn't Luke's handwriting, which was small and scrunched and almost illegible on a good day. This handwriting was beautiful—neat and measured, and there were little loops on the tail-ends of the A's.

"To tell you the truth," said Samuel, looking around stealthily, "I've been curious about this note since it landed on the front desk."

"Let's read it!" said Franny brightly.

Samuel gave a stealthy glance toward the door, then opened the envelope and slid out a single sheet of folded paper.

"My fingerprints are all over this anyway, since I'm the one who delivered it," he muttered, unfolding the paper. On reading the note, his smile faded.

"What does it say?" asked Franny.

"See for yourselves." Samuel held the note up.

"*You've caused enough pain. It's time for you to face the music. I'm here in Blue Valley, and I'm coming for you*," Alice read aloud, without touching the note.

"What are you all doing in here?" Eve Berkely came into the room holding a laundry basket brimming with towels. "Samuel, you know the police said we should stay out of here until they've gone over the room."

"Oh, that's right," said Samuel, giving Alice a little wink as he dropped the note back into the trashcan and led the group out of the room.

"Sorry, Eve," said Alice. "We were just having a look."

"Trying to solve another mystery?" Eve asked, leading the way down the hall and out of Cobblestone Way cottage. "I've heard about you three. We're lucky you're on the job."

"Thank you," said Alice. "Eve, can you tell us anything about Dr. Darlington?"

"Hm. I can tell you she wasn't here much. She came and went a lot. These doctors are a busy group, though. She got in Tuesday night, went out early

Wednesday, came and went all day. Next thing we heard was that she'd drowned at the lake. Awful!"

"Do you have any idea who sent her that note? The one left at the front desk?" Samuel asked his wife.

"No," said Eve thoughtfully. "Although, now that I think of it, there was a young woman in the reception area on Wednesday morning, after Dr. Darlington went out. I'd been back in the dining room, putting another pot of coffee on as people came in for breakfast. She must not have rung the bell, because when I came back to the front desk, she was there, looking at the guest book."

"Did she book a room?" asked Alice, feeling the hairs on the back of her neck stand up.

"She asked about a room, but we're all booked for the conference. I told her the whole town's pretty full, what with it being a holiday weekend."

"What did this woman look like?" asked Owen.

"Bright green eyes," said Eve. "Very striking. Blond hair."

"The woman from the bookstore!" said Alice. "Was she about my height? Maybe in her late twenties?"

Eve nodded. "That's her."

"You saw her, too, Franny. She'd been in the shop when Alexandra was so rude to me, and again the next day."

"I remember," said Franny, nodding. "She was really nice."

"I suspect she left the note," Eve concluded. "It wasn't on the desk when I'd gone back to the dining room. But, it was there when I came back. And so was the girl."

"Maybe this green-eyed girl of ours wasn't so nice after all," said Owen, raising a brow.

"Any idea where she went after leaving here?" Alice asked the Berkleys as they all arrived back in the reception area.

"I expect she went right where I sent her—to the only place left to stay in town," said Eve. "To the campground. Out at the lake."

CHAPTER 9

"Hopefully one of the glamping tents was available," said Owen as they hopped on their bikes and began pedaling toward the lake—which lay a short distance down Phlox Street, not far from the Valley Inn and the heart of town. "I mean, what do you do if you arrive in town and can't find a hotel room? It's not as if most people go around with a tent and sleeping bags in the trunk of their car, just in case."

The campground at Blue Lake, aptly named the Cozy Bear Camp and Glamp, offered everything from rustic, out-of-the-way sites, where campers could wander off into the woods, pitch their own tents, and enjoy peaceful nights around a campfire, to all-inclusive glamping tents, complete with wood floors, comfortable cots, electricity, and nearby bathrooms stocked with fancy soaps, fresh towels, and plenty of hot water.

Harve and Sue Anderson owned the campground. Back before Sue had come along, it was just a group of small clearings for tents with a scattering of barbecue pits. But when Sue, a refined woman with impeccable taste, fell in love with the outdoorsy Harve, she'd brought along a few touches of her own, and now the Cozy Bear offered something for everyone—including the occasional black bear sightings plus gorgeous views of both the lake and the mountains.

The Cozy Bear was almost directly across the lake from the town dock and fishing shack. Sue and Harve's house was nearby, a little further around the western edge of Blue Lake, in a small cluster of pretty houses. Meanwhile, Ben and Luke's homes were down at the eastern tip of the lake. The whole thing was encircled by a street called Lake Trail—which had started out, many years ago, as an actual trail, but was now a one-lane asphalt road that branched off of Phlox and wove its way through the trees and around the lake.

Alice slowed her bike and put her feet down as they passed under the Cozy Bear entrance arch, which this time of year, was covered with flowering trumpet vine.

"Wow, look at this," said Owen, getting off his bike and pointing at a sign near the entrance. "Tonight, there's a gourmet five-course feast at six, a singalong at seven, and ghost stories around the campfire at nine."

Franny walked over and looked at the sign. "Oh, my gosh. They have a moonlit canoe ride tonight and a guided hike in the morning. And, look at that yurt over there! I want to *live* here!"

"That's what all our customers say," said Harve Anderson, coming out of the small, stacked-log office building. "What brings you all out today?"

"Hi, Harve," said Alice. "Actually, we're looking for a guest of yours. A woman with bright green eyes and beautiful yellow-blond hair. Have you seen anyone who fits that description?"

"Are you three solving another mystery? Oh! I bet you're figuring out who that woman that died out here was!" Harve gave them a conspiratorial glance and lowered his voice. "Is this green-eyed woman connected to her somehow?"

"We don't know yet," Alice said, leaning closer to Harve. "But, we intend to find out."

"I know exactly the woman you're talking about, by the way. Those green eyes of hers are very unusual. She and her husband checked in Wednesday. They're in one of Sue's glamping tents, over that way. The one at the edge of the water." Harve pointed.

"So," Owen said in a loud whisper, "how are we going to approach the green-eyed monster? I mean, don't we need some kind of story, some kind of excuse—"

"Hello!"

Alice recognized the blond woman from the shop instantly. She was walking toward them, a broad smile on her face.

They all exchanged greetings and friendly smiles.

"I was just on my way to sign up for tonight's canoe ride, and then I saw you. You probably don't remember me," the woman said. "I was in your bookshop the other day. I love that place!"

"I do remember you!" said Alice.

"So do I," said Franny.

"I don't remember you, because I've never laid eyes on you before," said Owen. "I'm Owen James. My bakery, Sourdough, is right next to The Paper Owl."

"Of course! I was in Sourdough Wednesday afternoon, buying cupcakes. I talked to a nice woman with a German accent, I think?"

"Oh, she's not nice," said Owen. "She's the grumpiest woman on the planet."

"Oh, good. So, it wasn't me, then," the woman said with a relieved chuckle. "The cupcakes were amazing."

Owen glowed a little at the compliment. "Thank you! I'm glad you liked them."

"I'm Olivia, by the way. Olivia Nutley. My husband Seth is around here somewhere. It's our first time glamping, and we love it!"

"This is Alice, and that's Franny. She owns Joe's coffee shop," Owen said.

"Are you in town for the celebration?" asked Alice, not wanting the conversation to stall and Olivia to go on her way.

"No—well, sort of," said Olivia. "We wanted a little getaway, and we fell in love with Blue Valley the moment we saw it. It's just a lucky bonus that there's a celebration going on this weekend. We expected to find fireworks, but I hear there's a pretty big party out here at the lake tomorrow."

"Yep," said Alice. "On Main Street, all the shops and restaurants have decorations and specials. But, the main fun is out here. There's a huge cookout, a pie contest, kitschy carnival games and rides, and a boat parade with decorated kayaks, canoes, and pedal boats."

"Did someone say pedal boats?" A nice-looking man walked up and put his arm around Olivia.

"This is my husband, Seth," she said. "Seth, this is Alice—she owns the bookstore I was telling you about. This is Owen, who owns the bakery where I got the cupcakes. And, this is Franny—she owns Joe's coffee shop."

"Nice to meet you all," said Seth.

"And, I did say 'pedal boats', by the way," said Alice. "We have a whole fleet of them, over at the fishing shack." She pointed across the lake, where the little brightly colored boats could be seen, bobbing up and down in the water.

"I love pedal boats," said Seth. "We used to go out in them when I was a kid, at the park in the town where I grew up."

"There's even a pedal boat race," said Franny. "Tomorrow morning at eight."

"You should enter," said Owen.

"Could we?" asked Olivia.

"Sure," said Alice. "There's even an out-of-towners' division. It's the Blue Lake Independence Day Pedal Boat Regatta. My brother and I are entered."

"What she's not telling you is that she and her brother win it every year," said Owen.

"Not *every* year," said Alice, rolling her eyes.

"I've lived here for six years, and they've won it every single July since I've been going to that race," Owen countered.

"They're the local champs," Franny explained. "It's pretty competitive. Visitors can enter, too, and win things like gift certificates to local shops and restaurants and funky plastic trophies and stuff like that."

"Let's do it!" said Olivia, grabbing her husband's arm.

"Sounds like fun," Seth said. "How do we enter?"

"I can get you set up," said Alice. "My brother, Ben, is one of the people in charge of collecting names for the sign-up list. I'm going to his house right now. Just give me your contact information." She reached into her messenger bag and handed Olivia a small notepad and pen. Seth thanked Alice and excused himself, heading back toward their tent.

"Thank you! That is so kind of you," said Olivia, and Alice couldn't help but notice how genuine her smile was. "Blue Valley is the most hospitable town I've ever been to! Everyone's been so considerate."

Alice felt almost guilty. The Nutleys seemed to be

lovely people. Surely, this sunny woman wouldn't write a threatening note—much less kill anyone. Alice glanced at Owen and Franny, not sure how to proceed.

"So . . . Did you hear about the drowning out here at the lake Wednesday night?" asked Owen.

"Oh, yes," said Olivia. "We heard about it this morning. So terrible. To think of someone drowning—"

"It was the rude customer," Franny blurted out, interrupting.

"What?" Olivia looked confused.

"Remember the woman who was so rude when you were in my shop on Wednesday?" Alice watched Olivia carefully as she said the words.

"Of course," said Olivia, looking a little dazed.

"Sadly, she was the person who died here," said Alice, looking out at the water. She looked back at Olivia. "You look a little pale. You didn't know her, did you?"

"No," Olivia said quickly. "I mean, like I told you at the shop, I assumed she was one of the doctors in town for the conference. We tried to get a room at the Valley Inn before we came to the Cozy Bear, and the lady there said they were booked. We saw the conference attendants milling around—and they were all wearing matching lanyards. I remember the rude customer was wearing one, too."

"Well, you guessed right," said Alice. "She was one of the doctors from the conference. Alexandra Darlington."

There was a slightly awkward pause, then Olivia broke the silence, saying, "I'd better go find Seth." She moved away in the direction her husband had gone.

"Oh—don't forget to sign up for the moonlit canoe ride!" said Franny, pointing in the direction of the log cabin office.

Olivia immediately pivoted and headed that way. "Thanks for entering us in the regatta. We'll see you tomorrow morning," she said with a weak smile.

"Nice to meet you! See you tomorrow!" Owen called after her, waving.

"Well, she doesn't seem like a killer to me," said Franny.

"No way she's a killer," said Owen with a snort. "Too wholesome. What book did she buy, anyway? Hold on, let me guess: a romance novel? A YA fantasy? A book about how to crochet gifts for all your friends?"

"She bought an Agatha Christie book about a group of people on an island who are being killed off one by one."

"Ah." Owen cleared his throat. "Well, they do say you can't judge a book by its cover."

"Let's go over to Ben's," said Alice, turning her bike in the direction of her brother's end of the lake. "We're decorating the *Maelstrom* tonight, and Luke's bringing takeout from the Smiling Hound. It'll be fun."

"We can't," Franny answered, and Owen shook his head in agreement.

"Nope, we can't," he said.

"Why not? What's happening tonight?"

"Nothing!" said Franny, a little too quickly.

"What are you two up to?" asked Alice, suspicious. "I've never known either of you to turn down takeout from the Hound. Come on. We'll get a family-sized basket of onion rings."

Franny and Owen looked at each other and seemed to have an unspoken exchange of some kind.

"We really can't," said Owen. "Stuff going on at the bakery, you know. Plus, I want to go have a look at Alexandra's blog, see if there's anything else there."

"I was going to help him," said Franny. "I mean, with the bakery stuff."

"Oh. Okay, well, then, I guess I'll see you later tonight?"

"Yep!" Owen said, as he and Franny took the branch of Lake Trail that led back to Phlox Street.

"We'll see you tonight, after you get home!" called Franny.

Alice pedaled the rest of the way down Lake Trail to Ben's house and leaned her bike up against a tree. She walked toward the house, still wondering what her friends were up to.

"Good, you're here," said Ben, walking up from the lake. "I've got the decorations inside. We can get started while we wait for Luke to arrive with dinner."

"Oh—I have a new entrant for the regatta," said Alice, lifting the strap of her messenger bag over her head. She dug around inside the bag until she found the little notepad with Olivia's contact information. As Alice passed the notepad to Ben, she glanced down at the writing, and immediately snatched it back.

"Wait," she said, examining Olivia's handwriting. "But . . . They were so nice," she muttered.

"Who was so nice?"

"The Nutleys."

"The Nutleys? Alice, what are you talking about?" asked Ben.

"The A in *Olivia*. It has a little loop on the tail," said Alice, pointing at the note. "It's not obvious. But, it's there."

Ben frowned at Alice, then down at the note. Then, light dawned in his eyes. "You saw the note at the inn, didn't you? Samuel showed you the threatening note."

Alice nodded.

"That Samuel! You're not supposed to get involved in any more police business. You know that." Ben squinted at the lettering once more, then paused, then sighed. "Come inside. We're bagging this up."

CHAPTER 10

The Smiling Hound was famous with locals and visitors alike for its cozy atmosphere, friendly service, and delicious pub food. Countless bowls of hearty beef stew, baskets of thick-cut potato fries, and the juiciest burgers in town had been enjoyed there. Fish and chips, pot pies, gooey pizzas, and plates of mashed potatoes smothered in sausages and gravy were also on the menu—all served with a joke and a smile—and whether you liked your frosty mug filled with imported beer or root beer, you'd be sure to find something you liked at the Hound.

As the sun set over Blue Lake, Luke arrived at Ben's house with bags of food that smelled amazing.

"Just in the nick of time," said Alice, stepping out of the *Maelstrom*, onto Ben's dock. "We're starving."

"I guess getting a pedal boat in racing shape will do that to you," said Luke with a laugh. "It looks great!" He took a step closer and scrutinized the little boat. "I can honestly say I've never seen anything like it."

"Thanks," Ben said proudly, slinging an arm across his sister's shoulders. "We thought the serpent's head motif on the bow was a nice touch, even if it does make her a little less streamlined."

Luke nodded. "What's this symbol on the flag?" he asked, pointing to the flag which was attached to the stern end of the boat.

"That's the Helm of Awe," said Alice. "It symbolizes strength and protection. Viking warriors even carried amulets with this design—to protect them in battle."

Luke grinned at Alice the same way he always did when she started talking history. "You have a lot of good information stored in that head of yours, don't you?" he said. Then he leaned closer and gave her a peck on the cheek. "And a pretty head it is."

Alice felt her face growing warm—an effect Luke often had on her.

"If you're all done with the mushy stuff, let's eat," said Ben, eyeing the Smiling Hound bags.

"I got both your favorites," said Luke, setting the bags down on Ben's picnic table and unloading small containers filled with a selection of house specialties.

"Ugh, this hits the spot." Alice let out a happy groan as she bit into an onion ring.

Luke slid a small bundle wrapped in tissue paper her way.

Alice's looked at him with wide eyes. "The Crispy Turkey-Swiss Monte Cristo? I hardly ever let myself have one of these! How did you know this is my favorite?" She folded back the tissue wrapping to reveal a warm, golden-brown sandwich, lightly dusted with powdered sugar.

"I'm a detective, remember?"

"I'll never understand that sandwich," said Ben, shaking his head and taking an appreciative bite of his burger. "Who puts strawberry jam on a turkey sandwich?"

"*And* mustard and mayonnaise," said Alice. "Then, the whole thing is fried to crunchy perfection." She took a bite and closed her eyes to savor the balance of the flavors.

"I figured you'd want to carb-load before your big race tomorrow," said Luke. He paused for a few moments and looked from Alice to Ben. "So, how's the investigation going?" he finally asked.

"We're tracking down a few different leads," said Ben. "Of course, I can't talk about it."

"Oh, I know," Luke said quickly.

Ben looked at Alice and seemed to make a decision in his mind. "You know what? I'm going to run up to the house for just a minute. I'll bring us back a pitcher of tea."

"That sounds great!" said Alice, thankful to her brother for giving her a moment alone with Luke.

When Ben had gone, Luke took Alice's hand. "I want to talk to you. About Alexandra, and why I didn't tell you she was here," Luke said quietly.

"I know. And, I want to talk to you, too. But, we only have a few minutes before Ben comes back, and I need to tell you what happened today. It seems someone other than you didn't think too highly of Alexandra. Someone here in Blue Valley. A note was left for her at the Valley Inn—a threatening note."

"You saw the note? How? Do the police have it?"

"Samuel Berkley. He owns the Valley Inn. He let us see it before the police got there. They have the note now. Anyway, Eve—that's Samuel's wife—told us that a young woman had stopped by the inn right around the same time the note was left. The Berkleys didn't technically see her leave the note, but we decided to follow the trail, just in case. We found the young woman right over there." Alice pointed to the western end of the lake. "At Cozy Bear Camp and Glamp."

"Did you—" Luke, who was leaning forward tensely cleared his throat and sat back. "I mean, you met this woman?"

"She'd actually been in my bookshop Wednesday at the same time as Alexandra. She has these unusual bright green eyes. Anyway, when the Berkleys described her, I knew it had to be the same woman.

So, Owen, Franny, and I went over to Cozy Bear and found her."

"And?"

"She's really nice, actually." Alice couldn't help the tinge of disappointment in her voice. She wished Olivia had turned out to be even a little bit nasty.

"What does your instinct tell you, Alice? Your gut is usually right."

"My gut is undecided. Olivia seemed genuinely shocked that it was Alexandra who'd died Wednesday night—which would lead one to believe she didn't kill her. But then, I got her to write down her contact information so we could enter her and her husband in tomorrow's pedal boat race. Luke, the handwriting is similar to the handwriting on the threatening note. It's not completely obvious. She would have had to have tried to disguise it. But I think . . ."

"Listen to your gut, Alice."

"I think Olivia might have left that note."

"Did Ben get all this?"

"Yep. He has both the threatening note from the inn

and the one Olivia wrote today. He's sending it in to be analyzed." Alice covered Luke's hand with her own. "The bottom line is, if Olivia turns out to be the one who wrote that note, that means someone who had a score to settle with Alexandra is right here on the lake."

"Where the body was found," Luke finished. "Good lead, Alice. Have I ever told you you'd make an excellent detective?"

"Yep."

"Well, it's true." He looked at her and smiled appreciatively, then leaned forward and kissed her gently. "Sorry I've been a little out of touch these past few days. I really miss taking walks with you. Having lunch with you . . . Just little things like that. I've been laying low, I guess."

"You okay?"

"I'm a little shaken," he admitted. "It's not as though there was any love lost between Allie and me, but it's still disconcerting to see a person you knew . . ."

Alice nodded in understanding. "Of course, it is. I

wouldn't want you to be the kind of person who felt nothing in a situation like this."

"I also miss work. I'm ready to get back to it. I mean, I'm doing desk work, but it's not the same. Having Finn home helps a lot." He grinned. "Seeing you helps a lot, too."

Alice noticed his beard stubble was getting thicker, and his dark hair was a bit disheveled—a definite departure from his usually tidy appearance. She privately thought he might even be more handsome this way and found herself wondering what Luke Evans looked like when he first woke up in the morning.

"Tea, anyone?" Ben set a tray with a pitcher of tea and three glasses full of ice on the picnic table.

"Thanks," said Alice, pouring herself a glass.

"I had an interesting chat with Patrick when I picked up the food," said Luke, taking the pitcher.

Patrick Sullivan owned the Smiling Hound and was always glad to greet his customers and catch up on local goings-on. In fact, Patrick probably knew more about what was happening and who was seen where and with whom than anyone else in town. If you wanted the local scoop, Patrick was your man. Even Jane Elkin, owner, editor, and reporter for the *Blue Valley Post* often checked with Patrick when she was doing investigative reporting for an article.

"He told me he saw Alexandra Wednesday night," Luke continued.

Alice and Ben both sat up straighter.

"I don't like gossip, you know that," Ben said.

"We know," Alice assured him. "Go on."

"Patrick said Alexandra was at the Hound almost until closing Wednesday night. She was flirting with Norman McKenzie."

"*Norman*? Pearl Ann's gentleman caller?" Alice pictured the tall, lanky man who'd been dating Pearl Ann Dowry, owner of the Blue Beauty Spa on Main Street, since the fall. "Was Norman flirting back?"

"Patrick only said that they'd been sitting at the bar, talking, and then when Alexandra left, she was a little drunk—and she left with Norman."

"And that was just before she died," said Ben. He

looked at Luke, sighed, and finally said, "Zeb thinks she died somewhere around midnight, although he can't be a hundred percent certain. We're still waiting on the final word from the ME."

"So, maybe Alexandra somehow decided to take a midnight swim in the lake after drinking too much?" Luke scoffed. "I mean, that just doesn't sound like her."

"It doesn't sound like Norman, either," said Alice. "He's such a nice man. It's not like him to pick up a drunk woman at a pub."

"But, it does bear looking into," said Ben. "We have to remind ourselves that we don't always know people as well as we think we do."

Alice's eyes drifted back over to Luke, who met her gaze with a steady one of his own. "Alice, I didn't have anything to do with Alexandra or her death. She came to my cabin Wednesday morning, and that was the last I saw of her. I didn't tell you about it because, well, I wanted to forget it even happened. And, the headache I had that night? That was the worst stress headache I've ever had. I went to bed early. If she drowned right out there—"

"She didn't drown." Alice didn't mean to say it. She knew she wasn't even supposed to *know* it. But, she couldn't help it.

"What?" Luke looked shocked.

"Alice!" Ben scolded.

"I . . .I didn't mean—" Alice looked at Ben, then back at Luke.

"No, no," said Luke, getting to his feet. "I understand. You can't say anything else. It's okay." He turned to go, but then stopped and turned back. "I'm just glad to know you're on the case and making progress. I know you'll get to the bottom of this mess."

Alice couldn't tell in the evening light whether Luke was looking at her or at Ben—most likely, he was looking at both of them.

"Thanks for the dinner!" Alice called to Luke's retreating form. He gave a little wave but didn't look back again. "He hardly touched his food," she said, looking at Luke's half-eaten sandwich. "I'm worried about him."

"Me, too," said Ben. "This is an emotional roller

coaster for a man who rarely cracks. But he's holding it together."

"I'm glad he has Finn back."

"Me, too."

"I know he didn't kill anyone."

"Me, too."

Alice and Ben sat in silence a few moments longer, looking at the *Maelstrom* in all its glory.

"We'd better call it a night," Ben finally said. "Big day tomorrow. I'll see you here at seven, so we can warm up and pedal over to the starting line. By the way, I miss Franny and Owen being here tonight. I figured they'd join us—help us decorate the old girl."

"Me, too. They were very mysterious about what they're up to this evening," said Alice.

"Hmm."

"I'm sure they'll be at the race in the morning to cheer us on."

CHAPTER 11

"Okay, you two. Spill it."

Alice had come home from Ben's to find Owen and Franny in the garden, huddled around Owen's laptop.

"What?" asked Franny, a look of wide-eyed innocence on her face.

"Nice try, with the doe eyes there, Franny, but I'm on to you. What are you up to? I know you, and I know you'd never miss a lakeside feast from the Smiling Hound for nothing. And spending time with Ben. I had to eat extra onion rings, and now I'm all bloated." Alice turned to look Owen in the eye. "Out with it, Owen."

"Don't give me your stink eye, Alice. My lips are sealed."

"So, you admit you're hiding something!" said Alice, pointing an accusing finger at Owen.

When neither Franny nor Owen responded, Alice crossed her arms and said, "Fine. Don't tell me, then."

"If you must know, we're working on a project," said Franny.

"Franny!" said Owen.

"I can't help it!" said Franny. "I can't handle Alice's stink eye!"

"Go on," said Alice, trying to intensify her glare.

"That's right!" said Owen, putting an arm around Franny. "We're working on a small project!"

"What kind of project?"

"Never mind," said Owen. "We'll tell you tomorrow. Meanwhile, don't you want to hear what we found out from studying Alexandra's blog?"

This caught Alice's full attention. "You learned something new?"

"We'll show you," said Franny, scooting over so Alice could sit.

"Also, we've been waiting for you to get here so we could try these beauties," said Owen, opening a bakery box with six tiny cakes inside. "I see no reason why we shouldn't sample a couple of prospective wedding cakes while we fill you in. We'll start with pumpkin-caramel-cinnamon."

"How am I going to fit any more food into my stomach tonight?" asked Alice with a groan. "I'm serious. On Monday morning, we're turning over a new leaf! Extra miles and clean eating!"

"Just try a bite," said Owen.

"Mmm. Tastes like fall," said Franny, taking a bite and getting a smear of frosting on her nose.

"That frosting on your nose is a maple chai buttercream," said Owen, biting into his own cake.

"It's so comforting," said Alice. "So warm."

But Owen frowned. "Nope, this isn't it," he said.

"Owen, you're being entirely too picky. *All* of these cakes have been outstanding," said Alice.

"Okay, look here," said Franny, scrolling through the *Alexandra's Adventures* archives. "Here's an entry dated a year ago this week. Alexandra writes about what she carries in her purse."

"*What's in my bag*," Owen said, rolling his eyes. "I mean, like we're really going to believe she carries around a stethoscope in that five-thousand-dollar designer purse!"

Alice marveled at the professional-quality of the photos, which featured a buttery leather purse, its contents scattered about and surprisingly color-coordinated.

"She made it look like the purse just spilled open," said Franny. "But the irony is, she probably took an hour to arrange it exactly the way she wanted it."

"I bet," said Alice. "I mean, the way that pack of bubble gum is just casually lying on her open passport so we can see that she's been all over the world, apparently while chewing gum, and—oh." Alice slumped back in her chair, stricken.

"What?" Owen squinted at the computer screen. "Oh."

"What?" asked Franny, looking back and forth between the other two.

"Right there," said Owen, pointing at the artfully arranged contents of Alexandra's purse.

Franny leaned forward, then used the mousepad to zoom in. "Ohhh."

Right in between a pair of sunglasses and an expensive lipstick—just under one of the keys on a designer keyring—was an open locket containing a small photo of Luke.

"Well, they were engaged this time last year," said Owen.

Alice sighed. "That was probably shortly before they broke up, since Luke moved here in October."

Franny gave Alice a sideways squeeze. "More cake," she said, looking at Owen.

"Yes!" Owen passed around the second sample, a decadent pistachio cheesecake topped with shaved dark chocolate.

"I need this cake in my life," said Franny.

"Owen, you've outdone yourself," said Alice.

"This isn't the one," said Owen. "Back to the drawing board."

"So, what was it about this *What's-in-my-bag* article you found so interesting?" asked Alice, looking back at the computer screen and trying to avoid letting herself hone in on Luke's photo.

"Oh—right!" said Franny, scrolling down to the bottom of the article. "It's actually in the comments section. See here, where PeachJam2033 responded to the article?"

Alice leaned forward and read aloud. "'*You should be careful with the things that you treasure. Someone could take them all away someday.*'" She leaned back again. "Wow, that's undeniably creepy."

"And, look here," said Owen, reaching over and scrolling to the bottom of the next blog entry—a look at what Alexandra had eaten for lunch that day. Alice caught sight of the picturesque array of fruits, vegetables, cheeses, and a rustic chunk of dark bread, with a glass of red wine and chocolate truffles for dessert. The comment Owen pointed to read, *Watch what you eat. You might get sick.*

"It goes on and on," said Franny. "Every post

Alexandra wrote for the whole year, right up until she wrote this one." She stopped scrolling and turned the laptop toward Alice.

"Oh, yes, I noticed this one when I was reading through the blog. *Mini-Vacay in the Smokies*. She wrote this just a few days ago. It's about her plans for her trip here."

"That was the last post she wrote, before—" Franny looked at Alice.

"And look," said Owen, scrolling down to the bottom of the article. "PeachJam2033 strikes again."

"'*See you in Blue Valley*,'" Alice read slowly. "Wow. I'd read lots of Alexandra's posts, but didn't think to read the comments. This is serious. This peach jam person could most definitely be our killer."

"Did Ben have any new information about the police investigation?" asked Franny.

"Now, you know Ben can't tell me about classified stuff," said Alice.

"Oh, right," said Owen with a snort. "Alice, we all know you can get that bird to sing when you need to."

"Actually, Luke did find something out, but . . ."

"But, what?"

"But, I hope it doesn't pan out," said Alice. "Luke talked to Patrick Sullivan tonight when he picked up our food at the Hound. Patrick told him that Alexandra had been there late Wednesday night. Drinking. A lot."

"Wednesday night—as in, the night she died," said Owen.

"The very same," said Alice. "In fact, according to the coroner, Alexandra was probably killed around midnight. Patrick said she left the pub about that time . . . with Norman."

"*Norman McKenzie?*" Owen said, standing so abruptly he almost knocked his chair over.

"No way!" said Franny. "He adores Pearl Ann!"

"That's why I don't want it to be true," said Alice.

Owen looked across the street at the Smiling Hound, where the rooftop garden lights still glowed merrily, and the chatter of the customers could be heard.

"We have to go over there," he said.

"It's Friday night. Half the town will be there," said Alice.

"Exactly," said Owen. "Norman and Pearl Ann go there every Friday night. We need to ask some questions."

"Plus, we can talk to Patrick. See if he remembers any other details about Alexandra that night," said Franny.

"I have an early boat race in the morning," said Alice, hesitating. "Ben will kill me if I show up tired."

"Tough tootsies," said Owen, picking up his empty cake box resolutely. "We've got a killer to catch."

CHAPTER 12

The Smiling Hound was the place to be on a Friday night in Blue Valley—for locals and tourists alike.

Patrick Sullivan greeted Alice and her friends as they came through the door. "Hold on, now. Shouldn't you be resting up so you can defend your title tomorrow morning?" he asked, giving Alice a playful nudge.

"It's in the bag, right Alice?" said Owen with a chuckle.

"Why are you chuckling?" Alice asked him. "The *Maelstrom* is all decked out and ready to win."

"Come into the bar," said Patrick. "The place is crowded tonight with it being both a Friday and a holiday weekend. You three doing good business across the street?"

"Sold a lot of coffee today," said Franny, taking a seat on one of the pub's comfortable barstools.

"I actually sold out of my special red, white, and blue cupcakes," said Owen. "Hilda's baking another batch as we speak."

"Does Hilda ever sleep?" asked Patrick.

"I suspect she might be one of the un-dead," said Owen. "But that's fine by me if it means she's willing to bake at all hours. It works out well. I bake before dawn in the mornings, and she usually takes over the kitchen in the evenings."

"Hey, guys, what can I get you tonight?" Taya Helms, Patrick's head bartender set a bowl of homemade salt and vinegar potato chips down in front of them.

"You might want to try our special Red, White, and Booze Rum Freeze," said Patrick, sitting down next to Alice.

"Or our strawberry lemonade," suggested Taya.

"We also have our blueberry slushy on the menu tonight," said Patrick.

"Oh! The one with the tiny flag sticking out of it?" asked Owen.

"The very same," said Patrick with a nod.

"I'll have that," said Owen.

"Make that two," said Franny.

"I'll have the lemonade," said Alice.

"Rebel," said Owen.

"Two blueberry slushies and one strawberry lemonade, coming up," said Tara. "And don't worry, Alice, I'll put a tiny flag in yours, too."

"So, if I know you three, I'd bet you're not just here for drinks," said Patrick, resting an elbow on the bar.

"You'd win that bet," said Owen, popping a chip into his mouth.

"We're sort of casually wondering what happened to Alexandra Darlington, the doctor who died Wednesday night," said Alice.

"Right after she left here," added Franny.

"I was shocked when I saw her picture in the *Post*," said Patrick, shaking his head. "Sad business."

"What was your impression of her?" Alice asked.

"Pretty. Smart. Drunk."

"Did you notice anything out of the ordinary that night?"

"She came in around nine-thirty with a group of doctors from the conference. They got more obnoxious as the night went on. Most of them had left within an hour or so. It was down to Alexandra and one other guy. I got busy up on the roof and lost track of them. When I came back down, the guy was gone, and I saw Alexandra talking to Norman McKenzie. Then, around midnight, they left together."

"Didn't that strike you as odd?" Alice asked, as Taya set two bright blue slushies and one icy lemonade down in front of them.

"Absolutely," said Patrick. "That's why I noticed it. Norman leaving with someone other than Pearl Ann is most definitely odd." He saw the front door opening again and stood. "You should ask Norman about it. He's up in the garden with Pearl Ann."

"They never miss a Friday night, you know," said Taya. "Sorry. Didn't mean to eavesdrop. It's just that Norman couldn't be involved in that woman's death. He's a good guy."

"I don't think so, either," said Alice.

"How well do we really know Norman?" Owen whispered after Taya had moved on down the bar to attend to other customers. "I mean, what do we know about him other than the fact that he dates Pearl Ann?"

"Nothing, really," Franny admitted. "We know he's the best handyman in Blue Valley."

"He is?" asked Owen.

"Yep. Haven't you heard his ads on the radio?" said Alice.

"Norman is *Odd Job Bob*?" Owen's eyes widened.

"Yep," said Alice.

"I didn't realize," said Owen. "Why call himself *Bob*?"

"The original Odd Job Bob was Bob Davis," Alice explained. "When he retired, Norman became the new Bob."

"We should go up there and question him," said Owen. "But, with Pearl Ann sitting right there, he's not likely to open up about his late-night escapade with another woman."

"Owen! I'm sure it wasn't an *escapade*!" said Franny. She took a large gulp of her slushie. "Ow! Brain freeze!"

"Me, too!" said Owen, a pained expression on his face. "But, even though it's excruciating, I can't stop drinking this thing." He took another swig, then grabbed his forehead. "The agony!"

"Look. There's probably some logical explanation for the whole incident with Norman and Alexandra. We just need to find out what it is."

"I know!" said Owen. "Franny and I will get Pearl Ann away from the table. You question Norman."

"Okay," said Alice, as they all rose and picked up their drinks. "How are you going to get Pearl Ann to leave the table?"

Owen and Franny looked at each other.

"I've got it!" said Owen. "Leave it to me. Franny, drink up."

Franny nodded and they both drank more slushie, alternating between unabated enjoyment and the pain of the brain freezes. Then Owen set what was left of their drinks on the bar. "Let's go," he said.

"Hey, I'm not done with that yet!" said Franny.

"Yes, you are," said Owen. "To the roof!"

When they emerged into the Smiling Hound's rooftop garden—a charming space, strung with lights and scattered with small tables—they spotted Norman and Pearl Ann, sitting near the railing. Pearl Ann was enjoying a buttered ear of corn, and Norman was tucking into a multi-layered sandwich.

"Pearl Ann, we need your help!" said Owen, rushing up to the table.

"Oh, my gosh, what's happened to you?" said Pearl Ann with a little shriek. "Your lips are blue!"

"That's not the half of it!" said Owen. "Look at our teeth!"

He bared his blueberry-stained teeth, and Franny, catching on, followed suit.

"It's a spa emergency!" said Owen. "Please, tell me you have something for this!"

"What happened?"

"We'll tell you on the way to Blue Beauty," said Owen, grabbing Pearl Ann by the arm. "Norman, don't be alarmed," he said to Norman, who'd stood up, sandwich in hand. "We'll just borrow Pearl Ann for a few minutes. You chat with Alice here. Be right back!"

With that, Franny and Owen pulled Pearl Ann, who was still holding her corn, to the stairs and disappeared.

Alice turned back to Norman. "Don't worry. They'll be right back," she said, taking a seat. "I'll just keep Pearl Ann's chair warm." She laughed awkwardly, but Norman didn't seem to suspect anything was up.

"So, Norman," Alice said after clearing her throat several times and taking multiple sips of lemonade. "Can I ask you . . . I mean . . . Well, I'll just come right out with it."

"Go ahead," said Norman through a mouthful of sandwich.

"You were seen leaving here with the woman who died out at the lake on Wednesday night."

Norman coughed and a few breadcrumbs sputtered out of his mouth. "Oh. Sorry," he said, dusting off the table.

Alice could swear she saw a shadow of guilt cross Norman's face as he looked down over Main Street.

"That's okay," said Alice, hoping she was wrong.

"I read about that in the paper—that the woman died," said Norman. "Couldn't believe it. I mean, I didn't know her or anything. But it's strange, to see someone alive and well one night, and then hear they died."

"Very strange," Alice agreed. "Did you notice anything in particular about the woman?"

"Mainly that she was drunk," said Norman. "She was stumbling around all over the place, talking nonsense."

"Had you noticed her earlier in the evening? Like, who she was with?"

"She was with one of those doctors that's in town,"

said Norman. "Some guy. About her age. Dark hair. Short."

"Him, or his hair?"

"Him. Short and stocky."

"How did you know he was one of the doctors from the convention?"

"He had one of those nametag necklace things on."

"And then he left?"

"He stormed out. They'd been arguing. I wasn't trying to listen in, you understand. They were sitting about six feet away, talking pretty loudly. Anyway, I thought the guy was nuts. Was glad when he decided to leave. When the lady got up to go, she looked pretty woozy. I was leaving myself, so I offered to see her back to her hotel. But, then—well, I didn't."

"Why not?"

"She—" He stopped speaking abruptly and looked around. "This doesn't get back to Pearl Ann, you understand?"

"Of course," said Alice.

"She—" Norman stopped talking again, and the worried look on his face melted into a smile as he looked over Alice's shoulder toward the door.

Alice followed Norman's gaze and saw that Pearl Ann had returned with Owen and Franny, and was walking toward their table. Norman gave Alice a look and a very slight shake of his head that told her their discussion was over for the time being.

"You're a life saver, Pearl Ann," Owen was saying as Alice stood and Pearl Ann took her seat. "That was so embarrassing!"

"No problem," said Pearl Ann with a smile. "Now, don't forget to come in for your facials next week, you two. We'll get your pores shrunk down to nothing!"

"Will do," said Owen.

"Can't wait," said Franny.

"Well, we'd better be going now," said Alice, turning to go. "Early morning tomorrow."

Everyone nodded and said goodbye.

"Oh," said Alice, turning back. "I'm thinking of

stocking some homemade summer jams at the shop, and I'm taking a sort of informal survey. What are your favorite flavors of jam?"

"Without a doubt, mine's strawberry," said Pearl Ann. "I put it on everything!"

"Yum," said Alice. "And you, Norman?"

"Oh, that's an easy one," said Norman, picking his sandwich back up. "Peach. Most definitely peach."

CHAPTER 13

"Get anything out of Norman?" asked Owen as they made their way downstairs.

"He was just about to tell me something juicy when you got back," said Alice. "How'd it go with Pearl Ann?"

"Oh, it was so much fun," said Franny. "She had us do this honey-sugar lip scrub. Got the blue right off."

"And your teeth?"

"She had these little whitening sticks," said Owen digging into his pocket and pulling out what looked like a tube of lip balm. "You can take them with you to restaurants and things, for when you drink red wine. They get the stains right off."

"We got one for you, too, Alice," said Franny, unzipping a little pocket on her bag and handing Alice her own stain stick.

"Neat!" said Alice. "I had no idea such a thing even existed."

"I know, right?" agreed Owen. "By the way, you're going with us for facials next week. Your pores aren't in any better shape than mine."

"Gee, thanks, Owen."

"Don't mention it."

"Do you think Norman had anything to do with Alexandra's death?" asked Franny. "I mean, he did say peach jam is his favorite."

"That was pretty shifty, by the way—how you slipped that question in," said Owen, giving Alice a quick high-five.

"Thanks."

By that time, they were nearing the pub's exit.

"It sounds like Norman was just in the wrong place at the right time," said Alice. "I think he was legitimately worried that Alexandra was in danger because of the guy she'd been arguing with. Norman said the argument got pretty heated, and the guy left in a huff."

"Headed out?" Patrick held open the door as they approached.

"Yep," said Alice, but then she paused. "Hey, Patrick. Did you get a good look at the guy Alexandra was with last night? I mean, after the other doctors had all gone?"

"Sure, he just came in. He's right over there," said Patrick, raising his chin toward the bar. "Third from the left."

"Looks like our work here isn't done yet," said Owen, pivoting to walk back toward the bar.

"Is there a doctor in the house?" Owen snickered as he sat down at the bar at the end of a row of six men and women who were all wearing medical conference lanyards. "I jest," he said, holding up a hand.

Alice and Franny took seats next to Owen, and they ordered another round of slushies and lemonade from Taya.

"How did you know we're doctors?" one of the women asked.

"Those cute little nametags you're all wearing," said Owen.

"Oh, yeah," one of the men said, looking down at his lanyard. "We keep them on because a lot of businesses in town are offering discounts to conference attendees. All we have to do is show them these."

"Just our little way of showing we're glad to have you here in Blue Valley," said Taya, setting drinks down in front of Alice, Owen, and Franny.

"I'd like to offer you all a cup of free coffee at Joe's," said Franny.

"We might need it tomorrow morning," said one of the doctors, raising a glass.

"Hey, I'm going to run check on our table," the stocky, dark haired, third-from-the-left doctor said, getting up. He left the bar area and went into the pub's entryway, where Patrick and the restaurant hostess stood chatting.

Alice gave Owen and Franny a little nod, and said, "Be right back." She slipped off her stool, carrying her drink, and went in the direction of the entryway as well. As soon as she saw the doctor returning, she rushed forward, running into him and sloshing her drink on both of them.

"Oh! I'm so sorry!" Alice said, reaching out to blot the man's shirt with her cocktail napkin. "I'm such a klutz!"

The man, at first upset, softened considerably after he'd taken a better look at Alice. He laughed and said, "No problem. I was kind of hot anyway. Now I'm nice and . . . cool."

"And sticky," said Alice.

"Can I buy you a new drink?" he asked, looking at her half-empty glass.

"I'd better not," she said. "But, I can buy you one, to make up for your shirt."

"How about if you just join me for a drink instead?"

"Sure." Alice quickly spotted a small empty table in the bar area, tucked away into a corner. "How about over there?"

He looked with approval at the table and stepped aside so Alice could lead the way.

"I'm Steve, by the way. Steve Sander."

"Alice Maguire. I own The Paper Owl, just across the street."

"The bookshop? I'll have to stop in there before I leave town."

"I hope you do." Alice gave him her biggest smile—the one she reserved for occasions when she needed to make a customer she didn't know feel comfortable. She thought quickly about how to broach the topic of Alexandra. "So, how's the medical conference going so far?"

"Really well," Steve answered. "If you like talks about the latest pharmaceuticals, procedures, and insurance plans."

"Sounds . . . very interesting."

"Right." He laughed.

"Are you a surgeon, or—"

"I'm a general practitioner. Over in Bell Cove."

"I'm not sure—"

"Where that is?" Steve laughed. "That's because no one's ever heard of it. It makes Blue Valley look like a bustling metropolis." He waved at Taya, who came over and took his order.

Alice cleared her throat. "I was, um, sorry to hear about the doctor who died out at the lake," she said, watching Steve's eyes. "Was she a friend of yours?"

"Not really. I've met her before, you know, at doctors' things like this. But it's been years. I was shocked to see her at the conference."

"Oh, so you didn't know her well," said Alice, nodding and trying to formulate her next questions as artfully as possible. "Did you hear how she died?"

"Drowned, I assume," Steve answered. "She was pretty drunk that night. Alcohol and lakes don't mix well."

"I know it's, well, in poor taste to speak ill of the dead . . ." She looked at Steve, whose eyes widened in interest. "But, I heard she wasn't all that easy to get along with."

Steve sat back in his chair and took a swig of the beer Taya had set on the table. "You know what, Alice? That, I can believe."

Alice looked at him expectantly, encouraging him to go on.

"I had a pretty bad argument with her just the other night," Steve said.

"Really?" Alice's heart pounded. "What about?"

"Oh, medical stuff. Nothing, really. I felt bad when I heard she had died, because that was the last conversation I'd had with her."

"And, maybe even the last conversation she ever had," Alice added.

"No, I bet she found someone else to argue with after I left. In my experience, she was a very disagreeable woman."

Steve took another drink of beer.

"Hey, Steve, table's ready," one of the other doctors from their group said, walking up.

Steve looked regretfully at Alice. "Join us for a late dinner, Alice?"

"I'd better not," said Alice, getting up. "I have an early morning tomorrow."

"Well, it was nice to meet you," Steve said, lowering his voice and standing a little too close for Alice's comfort. "I'll come check out the bookstore sometime."

After the group of doctors had disappeared into the dining room, Owen and Franny hurried over to join Alice, and they finally left the pub.

"Let's walk a bit before we go home, okay?" Alice said, taking a deep breath of fresh air.

"Good idea," said Franny. "It's so nice out."

They headed further down Main Street, glancing into cheerfully lit shop windows and enjoying the blissful quiet after being in the noisy pub.

"What'd the good doctor have to say?" asked Franny.

"I bet he spilled his guts after you turned your womanly wilds lose," said Owen.

"My *what?*" Alice scoffed. "I assure you, no womanly wilds were set loose this night."

"Please. That man was flirting with you like there's no tomorrow."

"He was," Franny agreed.

"His name is Steve Sander. He's a small-town doctor. He was acquainted with Alexandra, but didn't seem to know her all that well," said Alice. "He said he was surprised to see Alexandra here, and admitted they'd had a pretty heated argument the other night."

"About?" Franny perked up.

"A medical issue."

"Darn," said Franny.

"Borrring," said Owen.

"Meanwhile, Norman admitted he left the pub with Alexandra, but said he failed to walk her all the way back to the inn."

"Why?" asked Franny.

"He didn't get to that part," said Alice.

"And then there's the peach jam issue," Franny reminded them.

"That's right. Peach jam," said Owen. "Could Norman be the creepy commentator on Alexandra's blog?"

"There's his car," said Alice, pointing to where Norman's old yellow pickup truck was parked in front of the Blue Beauty Spa. "Let's take a peek inside. Just in case."

They all attempted to act casual as they strolled around Norman's truck, nonchalantly glancing into the windows. Unfortunately, the truck was neat as a pin inside. There was nothing on the seats or the floorboards, as far as they could tell.

"I mean, what were we expecting to find?" Owen said, stepping back onto the sidewalk in front of the spa. "A meat cleaver or something?"

Franny gave a little laugh. "It's seriously getting late now. Let's go home," she said.

"Uh-oh," said Alice, still looking at Norman's truck.

"Uh-oh, what?" said Owen.

"We were looking *in* the truck. Not *on* it," said Alice, pointing at the back tires.

"Ew," said Owen, wrinkling up his nose. "Is that where the stinky smell is coming from?"

"What's that caked all over the tires?" asked Franny.

"I'd know that mud anywhere," said Alice.

"Smells familiar," said Franny. "I've got it! It's from the lake!"

CHAPTER 14

"You look awful!" Franny said when she saw Alice early the next morning.

"Coffee!" Alice said in a moan. She'd just dragged herself out into the garden after her alarm clock hit the floor for the second time that week—this time, because Alice had literally only fallen asleep forty-five minutes earlier and had been dreaming that someone was shrieking at her in a high-pitched, obnoxious way. So, she'd instinctively whacked at the thing making the noise.

She plopped down into her chair and reached cautiously up to touch her hair, finding it had grown exponentially in the July humidity, and cursing herself for leaving the windows open overnight. Now, her head resembled a big, red, frizzy ball.

"This should help," said Franny, filling Alice's mug.

After her first sip, Alice became aware that it was a glorious morning. The rooftop garden, touched with silvery dew, was gleaming in the sun as it crept over the mountains. Early morning tourists could already be seen, moving around on Main Street, walking down to the Parkview Café, Crumpets, or Sourdough to find breakfast before the day's events got underway.

"Oh, my. You have bags under your bags," said Owen, taking a look at Alice after coming out of his apartment smelling like fresh-baked bread. He set a still-warm cinnamon raisin loaf on the table.

"Thanks, guys," said Alice, taking another long drink of coffee and helping herself to a thick slice of the bread. "I was up almost all night."

"You were supposed to hit the hay after we came home!" said Franny.

"I did. But, I couldn't sleep, thinking about Norman .

. . and Dr. Steve . . . and Alexandra . . . and peach jam." Alice shook her head dolefully, then laid it down on the table. "My head weighs a ton."

Poppy hopped up and swatted at Alice's hair.

"Cut that out, Poppy," said Alice. "I texted Ben, by the way, to make sure he knew about Alexandra's argument with Dr. Steve. He said they'd questioned Steve and that he's no longer a suspect. Seems he'd claimed to have returned to the inn by eleven that night, and witnesses corroborated that. So, he's not our killer." Alice yawned. "I finally gave up trying to sleep, got up, and read through Alexandra's blog again. I didn't even go back to bed until a little while ago."

"Find anything new?" Owen asked.

"I think I might have." Alice scrolled through her phone until she found what she was looking for. "I was reading the comments again, on the blog posts. Did you notice there were times when PeachJam left more than one comment on a single post?"

"No," said Franny, coming around the table to peer over Alice's shoulder at the phone.

"Sometimes, if you scroll further down through the comments . . ." Alice pointed to the screen.

By this time, Owen was peering over Alice's other shoulder. "'*I hate you, Alexandra! You have absolutely zero cellulite, and you make me sick!*'" he read.

"What? No, not that one." Alice squinted at her phone. "This one."

"'*Doctors are supposed to be healers. Not killers,*'" Franny read. "Oh wow. We missed that one because PeachJam had made a more recent comment, up near the top. We didn't think to scroll further down through all of these."

"Did Alexandra not vet the comments on her blog?" Owen scoffed, sitting down in his chair. "I mean, what kind of social media suicide is that? Everyone knows you censor the comments!"

Alice and Franny looked at him.

"Owen, I had no idea you were so savvy," said Franny.

"You censor the comments on the Sourdough blog?" Alice asked.

"Of course."

"So, that time when you were making those licorice-filled pastry puffs, last October . . ." Alice raised an eyebrow at Owen.

"Ah, yes. The licorice puff debacle," said Owen, rolling his eyes. "You're darn right I censored those comments. People were actually leaving those little barf emojis." Owen dusted an imaginary crumb off his shirt. "I only kept the nice remarks. Like when Bea said she couldn't wait to try them."

"Bea? As in my mother?" Alice asked.

Alice never ceased to be surprised that Owen had a whole fun relationship with her parents that she never knew anything about until he'd mentioned something like going birdwatching with her father or baking cookies with her mother. Hearing that her mother followed and commented on Owen's blog—or *any* blog for that matter—was a bit of a shock.

"Of course. Bea's my biggest fan," said Owen.

"You're her favorite. I know it," said Alice with a sniff.

"Now, now," Owen said in a comforting tone. "It's not a contest, Alice."

"*As we were saying*," Franny interjected, getting back to the subject at hand. "PeachJam said doctors are supposed to heal people. Not kill them."

"Right," said Alice.

"When did they make that comment?" asked Owen.

"A year ago. This was the first post PeachJam commented on—the *What's-in-my-bag* post."

"So last July . . ." said Owen, taking out his phone. "Which hospital did Alexandra work at?"

"Tennessee General, Nashville. In the ER," Alice said, scratching Poppy behind the ears.

"Let's see here," Owen tapped away at his phone, scanning and scrolling as he went. "Here we go," he said finally. "Obituaries for this time last year in Nashville. Seems like there weren't all that many deaths that month . . ."

"You might be on to something," said Alice, pulling up the obituaries on her own phone. "Maybe

PeachJam was angry at Alexandra because they'd lost someone they loved in her ER."

"That makes sense," said Franny, taking out her phone as well.

They all scrolled and studied in silence for a time.

"How will we know which one of these is connected to PeachJam?" Franny finally asked.

"Look at who the deceased was survived by," said Alice. "Look for any information about where they died and who they left behind."

"I'm also checking the hospital data," said Owen. "Seems like Tennessee General has an excellent record."

"Hold it!" Alice sat up straight in her chair. "Ethel Grant, died July 2, last year—two days before PeachJam made that comment. Age eighty-nine. Heart attack."

"Not to sound callous, but that seems like a pretty natural death," said Owen.

"'Survived by her devoted granddaughter, Olivia

Grant-Nutley.'" Alice set the phone on the table and looked at her friends with wide eyes.

"Oh. My. Gosh." Owen picked up Alice's phone and re-read the notice.

"The Olivia Nutley we met at the campground?" Franny asked.

"The Olivia Nutley who was so nice?" Owen added, looking disappointed.

"The Olivia Nutley who's handwriting looked like the handwriting on the threatening letter in Alexandra's room at the inn!" said Alice.

"What? Really?" asked Owen. "Why didn't you tell us this sooner?"

"I was so busy trying to figure out what you two were up to, and then we went to the Smiling Hound, and I completely forgot. Besides, I can't be sure. It all comes down to a little loopy thing on the letter A. The notes are being compared by an analyst."

They all sat in stunned silence for a moment, sipping coffee and eating cinnamon raisin bread.

"We need to recap, because my brain is starting to

overload," Owen said finally. "First, we know Norman's recently been at the lake—because of the stinky mud on his tires."

"*And* he was seen with Alexandra right before she died—and, her body was found at the lake," added Franny.

"Then, there's Dr. Steve," said Alice. "We know he argued with Alexandra the night she died."

"And that he has the hots for you," said Owen.

Alice scowled at Owen. "But, we also know Dr. Steve said he was back at the inn around eleven, and Alexandra didn't die until after midnight."

"Let's keep him on the list anyway," said Owen. "For all we know, he's a murderous sleepwalker."

"Right," said Franny. "We know that Olivia Nutley—"

"Who may turn out to be an *actual* nut—" Owen interjected.

"May be PeachJam-whatever and may feel that Alexandra killed her beloved grandmother."

"Almost exactly a year ago," Owen finished. "It's not

looking good for Olivia."

"I'm late," Alice said, checking the time on her phone. "We'd better get over to the lake. Franny, bring the coffee."

Blue Lake was shimmering in the sunlight as Alice, Franny, and Owen pedaled their bikes through the trees along the winding Lake Trail to Ben's house.

"There you are!" Ben said when he saw his sister walking down to the water's edge where the *Maelstrom* bobbed at the edge of the dock. "And Owen and Franny, too!" Ben jogged over to his fiancé and gave her a kiss on the cheek. "Here to cheer us on?"

"Oh, yes," said Franny, patting Ben on the back.

"We're here for *many* reasons," Owen added.

Ben gave the three of them a skeptical look. "What are you up to?"

"We have an idea about who killed Alexandra," said Alice.

"We have *many* ideas," Owen added.

"We're trying really hard to narrow them down," said Alice. "We've been reading Alexandra's blog—"

"You'll have to tell me about it on the way," said Ben, glancing at his watch. "We're already late, and we still have to paddle down to the town dock."

"We'll meet you there!" said Franny, giving Ben a quick peck.

She and Owen jogged off through the trees in the direction of the town dock.

Alice glanced at the little walking path that led from Ben's house to Luke's cabin. "I wonder if Luke's coming," she said.

"He'll be at the race," Ben assured her, holding the boat steady as Alice climbed in. "Tell me your ideas about the case."

By the time they pulled up at the town dock, where starting-line banners were flapping in the breeze, Alice had filled Ben in on their three main suspects.

"I should have the results of the handwriting analysis

any time now," said Ben. "Do you see the Nutleys anywhere?"

Alice scanned the various contestants, climbing into pedal boats bedecked with flags and streamers. She quickly caught sight of Olivia's sunflower-colored hair. She and Seth were getting into their boat on the visitors' side of the dock.

"There they are," Alice said, subtly pointing them out.

"Good. We'll keep an eye on them, just in case."

"Look—there's Mom and Dad!" said Alice, pointing to where Martin and Bea Maguire were standing on the dock, waving furiously and snapping photos of their children. Alice and Ben smiled and waved back.

"Enough socializing. Let's size up our competition," Ben said, as he and Alice scanned the locals who'd entered the race.

"There's Norman and Pearl Ann," said Alice. "Oh, my gosh! That explains the mud on Norman's truck tires."

"Sure does," said Ben. "They're in a custom pedal boat. Norman would have hauled it over here yesterday and probably backed up to the boat launch in his truck."

"Look. Their boat is called the *Pearl Ann*," said Alice. "There's even a special seat for Polly! How sweet is that?" Pearl Ann's corgi, Polly, looked perfectly content, seated in her cushioned nest between Pearl Ann and Norman.

"Who else is entered this year?"

Ben and Alice looked down the line of pedal boats. They saw Faith Lindor, who owned Crumpets, and her fiancé Beau—who might've been stiff competition, but their boat looked old and slow. Marge Hartfield, who'd named her boat *Flicker* in honor of her passion for candle making, was sharing a boat with Koi Butler, the town's favorite yogi. But, Marge wasn't what you'd call an athlete, and Koi looked like he was having too much fun rocking their boat to take the race seriously. Next were the Whitmans, who owned the local grocery store. They were an older couple and unlikely to pose a threat.

"Wow, look at that boat," Alice said, leaning to see down the row where a gleaming pedal boat bobbed in its slot.

"What's it called? The . . . The *Valkyrie*?" Ben abruptly stood, rocking the boat and almost falling over. "My gosh, Alice! It's a work of art!"

Alice stood up as well, to get a better look. "Who else besides us would name their boat for Viking mythology?"

"The Valkyries . . ." Ben said thoughtfully.

"Odin's own maidens," muttered Alice.

"Would you look at that? It's a Sailfish. That's the nicest pedal boat in existence. It's got a kick-up rudder system, double sun shade, extra-large, built-in cooler compartment, and non-slip pedals. Look at that shine! That's high-density polyethylene, Alice!"

"Oh, for the love of . . . We're in trouble."

"Who—"

At that moment, Alice and Ben saw their opponents boarding the *Valkyrie*.

"Franny? And Owen!" Alice let out a gasp.

"They're in the race? Since when? When did they register?"

At this point, Owen had spotted them gaping, and gave them a friendly wave as he helped Franny into the boat. When Franny peered over the other boats and saw Ben and Alice, she smiled and blew a kiss to Ben.

"So that's what they've been up to!" said Alice.

"They've secretly been plotting against us!" said Ben, sitting down and gripping the rudder. "Just look at them over there. So confident. You can tell they think the Champion's Cup is theirs."

Alice sat down and put her feet snugly onto the pedals. "Not today," she said through gritted teeth.

"Hey, Alice!"

Alice turned and saw Luke, standing on the shore with Finn, who was furiously wagging his tail, by his side.

Alice waved back happily. "Luke looks better today. More rested, don't you think?"

"Focus, Alice," Ben warned.

"Get ready, everybody!" Mayor Abercrombie was standing at the end of the town dock, holding a megaphone and a bullhorn. "Now, I want a fair, clean race. No horseplay out there."

"Why is he looking at us?" asked Ben.

With that, the mayor sounded the bullhorn, and the row of pedal boats were off, moving out into the lake toward the bright orange buoys near the middle, where they would turn and head back to the finish line.

Alice and Ben took an early lead but were slowed down a bit when the Whitmans accidentally pedaled into them. Pearl Ann and Norman were too busy laughing and yelling greetings to the other boats to get up much speed. Faith and Beau were a force to be reckoned with until they lost their rudder and ended up having to paddle home using their emergency oar—a necessity that disqualified them from winning.

It came down to the *Maelstrom* and the *Valkyrie* for the win. Alice and Ben pedaled with all their might. Alice's legs were burning from the effort. Owen and Franny edged out in front, and as they all neared the shore—the crowd going wild—Finn started barking furiously, dragging Luke away from Zeb Clark, who he'd been chatting with, into the shallow water at the edge of the lake. Alice saw this, and her heart melted. Finn had recognized the *Maelstrom* and was trying to get to it. He remembered Alice and Ben! The distraction was enough to cause Alice to lose her edge, and Owen and Franny drove the *Valkyrie* home to victory.

"The Maguires have been toppled, after winning this regatta seven years straight! The Champion's Cup passes into the hands of Franny Brown and Owen James! Be sure to come again next year because all bets are off!" Mayor Abercrombie announced, then added, "Everyone, go enjoy the carnival and food—and bring your blankets and lawn chairs out tonight for fireworks over the lake!"

A few moments later, the mayor presented the cup to Owen and Franny, who waved graciously at the cheering crowd. Alice saw that the Nutleys had won a prize as well—a gift certificate from the Smiling Hound. Watching them accepting the award with genuine gratitude and excitedly hugging first the mayor and then one another, Alice found it hard to believe that Olivia Nutley was a cold-blooded killer. But, then, she also knew that people sometimes did crazy things for love.

Ben's cell phone buzzed, and he stepped aside. The

next thing Alice knew, he was walking quickly up to the Nutleys, and taking Olivia by the arm.

Alice felt her heart sink.

"Mrs. Nutley, I'm going to need you to come with me," Ben said, showing her his badge.

Olivia looked shocked at first, then furious, then she began sobbing.

Alice felt almost dizzy, between her sleepless night, the exertion of the race, and now, seeing Olivia being arrested.

"I guess the handwriting analysis came back," Luke said quietly, putting a supportive arm around Alice. A damp Finn sidled up and gave her calf a comforting lick.

As Ben escorted Olivia past them, Alice saw a defeated look in Olivia's eyes.

"She killed my grandmother," she was tearfully saying to Ben. "That horrible woman killed my grandmother, and she didn't even care! She deserved what she got."

"I'm sorry," Ben said, keeping his voice low, not

wanting to cause a scene. "Let's talk about it at the station."

He glanced back at Alice and Luke, and then disappeared among the trees.

Alice looked around and found Seth in the crowd, looking completely dumbfounded, still holding the Smiling Hound gift certificate in his hand.

CHAPTER 15

Owen and Franny, their arms loaded with giant bags of cotton candy, popcorn, and various types of deep-fried foods on sticks, came and joined Luke and Alice.

"Can you believe this? Vendors are giving Franny and me free goodies," Owen said, waving a corndog. "The spoils of victory!"

"I got a deep-fried candy bar for Ben," said Franny. "Where'd he go?"

"Probably sulking because the *Maelstrom* couldn't defeat the *Valkyrie*," said Owen.

"He's gone to the station," Alice said. "He took Olivia

Nutley in for questioning."

"What?" Franny dropped her candy bar. "Oops."

"Olivia's the killer after all?" said Owen, his shoulders sagging a little. "I'd kind of decided she was innocent. Are we sure about this?"

"But, she's so nice," said Franny.

"Ben just received the results of the handwriting analysis. Olivia wrote the threatening note. And, she's got to be PeachJam. As they were leaving, I heard her say Alexandra deserved to die—that she had killed Olivia's grandmother," said Alice.

Owen gave a little whistle. "Well, that is pretty damning."

"Now that Olivia's in custody, I'll tell you that I had another chat with Zeb this morning while we were watching the race," said Luke. "His theory is that Alexandra was hit by a car before she was tossed into the lake. I'm sure one of our officers is headed over to the campground to examine the Nutleys' car right now."

"That explains the strong impact part of the story," said Alice.

"I suddenly don't feel like riding the Ferris wheel," said Franny, looking deflated.

"Let's go home," said Owen. "We're none-too-fresh after that race. We can get cleaned up and come back out to the lake later on."

"Good idea." Alice felt a wave of exhaustion wash over her after the stress of the past few days coupled with two nights in a row with precious little sleep. She gave Finn a pat on the head and Luke a kiss on the cheek. "I'm sorry for Olivia. Sorry for Alexandra, too. But, I'm so relieved your name can be cleared now."

"Once the details are hammered out, yes. I hadn't even really let myself think that far," said Luke, wrapping his arms around Alice and pulling her close. She felt his body relax and when he looked at her again, she noticed his smile had lost the tight tension of the past few days. "So glad it's almost over," he said. "Thank you for your help." He looked at Owen and Franny. "All of you."

"Fresh start?" asked Alice, grinning.

Luke took her hand and kissed it. "Finally."

. . .

"I wonder what Norman was going to say last night, when I talked to him at the Hound," Alice said as they walked their bikes up Phlox Street toward Main.

"That's right. You said he was about to tell you something important when we walked up," said Franny.

"Guess it doesn't matter now," said Owen, tilting his head toward the police station as they passed it. "Now that they've probably got the killer in custody."

"Do you two really, in your heart of hearts, think Olivia ran over Alexandra, hauled her out to the lake, and dumped her in?" asked Alice, stopping.

"You read my mind," said Franny. "That's just not sitting right in my gut."

"Could be the fried pizza-on-a-stick you just had for breakfast," said Owen. "I mean, we know Olivia wrote that note, and I assume she wrote the comments on *Alexandra's Adventures*. Even if she was rightly upset about her grandmother, those aren't the actions of an innocent person."

"You're right," said Alice, nodding as they turned onto Main Street.

"Yep. You're definitely right," agreed Franny.

"But still . . ." said Alice, slowing her pace again. "What was Norman going to say last night?" She looked at Owen and Franny. "I'm sorry, guys. I just feel like something's off. Like the puzzle is still missing a piece or two."

"Well, there's Norman's truck, right over there," said Owen, pointing up Main to where the yellow truck was parked, with the *Pearl Ann* loaded in the back. "We could talk to him one more time."

"And look! There's Norman!" said Franny.

Sure enough, Norman was just exiting the Blue Beauty Spa, headed toward his truck. Alice, Owen, and Franny hopped onto their bikes and pedaled up just as Norman was digging his keys out of his pocket.

"Hey, Norman! Hold up a second!" called Owen.

"Hey! Good race today, everybody," Norman said with a smile.

"You, too, Norman," Alice said, gesturing toward the pedal boat. "The *Pearl Ann* is lovely."

"Thanks. It was a surprise for Pearl Ann," he said. "You all going to the fireworks tonight?"

"Wouldn't miss it," said Alice. "Hey, Norman . . . Remember last night at the pub, when you were about to tell me what happened after you and Alexandra left there Wednesday night? I'm so curious. Could you tell us the rest of that story now?"

"I, uh—" Norman looked nervously back and forth between the three of them, then sighed and said, "Well, it's embarrassing, but I guess you might as well know." He glanced toward the spa. "Pearl Ann doesn't need to know about this, okay?"

Alice, Owen, and Franny all nodded rapidly.

"Okay. I'll make this quick. The lady—Alexandra? She was pretty upset after that argument with the other doctor. She'd clearly had too much to drink and went stumbling out of the pub after a while, like I told you. I had this feeling she might be in danger—probably because the guy seemed so hateful when they were arguing. Anyway, now, I feel like her dying is partly my fault."

"Why would you think that?" asked Alice.

"If I'd done what I'd planned to do—which was to see her safely back to the inn—maybe she would've been all right. But she . . . well, she made a play for me."

"She *what*?" Alice hadn't meant to react with such surprise. Norman was a nice-looking man. But, he was well into his 60s, and not exactly what one might think of as the glamorous Alexandra's type.

"She made a pass at me, when we left the pub, halfway down Main Street." Norman had turned as red as a beet by this point. "All I could think about was how Pearl Ann wouldn't like it, so I pointed the lady toward the Valley Inn and left her there. Then, when I heard she'd died right after that, I felt awful."

"Oh, Norman, that's not your fault," said Franny, patting him on the back.

"Maybe not, but if I'd just walked her back, maybe whoever killed her would've left well enough alone. I don't know . . ." Norman rubbed the back of his neck.

"You said you felt Alexandra might be in danger . . . That the man she'd argued with seemed hateful. Did you happen to hear what they were arguing about?"

"Some of it. I heard him say something like, 'You're going to pay, Allie.' I remember that because I have a niece named Allie. Oh! He also said, 'You ruined me.'"

"You didn't hear them discussing anything about medical issues . . . doctor stuff?" asked Alice.

"Nope. It seemed more personal than professional." Norman opened the door to his truck and climbed in. "Sorry, kids. That's all I know."

"Thanks, Norman. You've been a big help," Alice assured him, as he put the truck in gear, gave them a wave, and drove off.

"He called us *kids*," said Owen. "Do you have any idea how long it's been since anyone's called me a kid?"

"Dr. Steve lied," said Alice. "He said that he and Alexandra hardly knew each other—that their argument was strictly medical."

"But remember, he was at the inn at eleven," said Owen. "Alexandra didn't die until an hour later."

"I can't believe I'm going to say this," said Alice. "But, we have to go back to the inn. We need to double check with the Berkleys."

CHAPTER 16

"To tell the truth, I'll be glad when these doctors check out tomorrow," said Eve Berkley, who was sweeping the front porch when Alice, Owen, and Franny rode up to the Valley Inn on their bikes. "Some of them are downright snotty. And the comings and goings! Our front drive is turning into an interstate highway!"

"Eve, we need to know about one of the doctors in particular," said Alice, leaning her bike against a tree. "Dr. Steve Sander? Do you know who he is?"

"Kind of short? Dark hair?"

"Bingo," said Owen. "That's the one."

Eve looked pleased with herself. "We do try to get to know every one of our guests here. Personalized service. That's what sets the Valley Inn apart."

"It certainly does," said Alice. "We were wondering . . . Dr. Sander said he came back to the inn around eleven on Wednesday night. Can you remember if that's true?"

"Oh, yes, the police asked that, too," Eve said. "I do remember Dr. Sander coming in at eleven, because I was just settling in to watch the eleven o'clock news."

"But, then, he went out again," said Samuel, who'd been watering the riot of colorful coneflowers, daisies, and butterfly weed that grew in the beds in front of the main inn house.

"What? No, he didn't," said Eve. She looked back at Alice. "Our little apartment is right there by the front desk. I always know when people come in and go. Dr. Sander was staying in the main house. He would've passed our door. He did not go by twice that night!"

"Yep, he did," said Samuel. "Around eleven forty-five."

"Did you tell the police that?" asked Franny.

"Nope, they never asked," said Samuel.

"That's because they asked me, you goof," said Eve. "I never saw Dr. Sander leave."

"Well, I did," said Samuel. "You fell asleep during the news, like you always do. I was watching the late show when I saw Dr. Sander walk out and get into his car."

"So, there's another lie from Dr. Steve," said Owen. "He lied about his whereabouts Wednesday night, *and* he lied about the nature of his argument with Alexandra."

"I'm still wondering why, exactly, Dr. Steve would kill Alexandra," said Franny. "I wonder what happened between those two."

"Hold on," said Alice a light dawning in her memory. "Norman said he called her Allie!"

"Annnd . . ." said Owen.

"That's what they called her back in med school! Luke told me," said Alice. "She hated that nickname!"

"Annnd . . ." Owen said again.

"Dr. Steve said he knew Alexandra from conferences and things. But, if he'd only known her in that capacity, he would never have called her Allie! I'm guessing this means he knew her in med school."

"Three lies and you're out, Dr. Steve," said Owen.

"So, they go way back," said Franny. "Something seriously horrible must've happened between them in the past."

"Norman said he heard Steve say, 'You ruined me,'" said Alice. She turned to the Berkleys. "Eve and Samuel, is Dr. Sander here now?"

"I don't think so," said Eve. "Pretty sure he left a while ago."

"He hasn't checked out or anything?"

"Oh, no," said Samuel. "The conference goes on through tomorrow. I expect he's gone into town. But, who knows? They come, they go. We can't keep track of them. We'll keep an eye out—let you know if we see him."

After thanking the Berkleys, Alice, Owen, and Franny walked their bikes through the picket fence gate and down the tree-lined drive that led out of the Valley Inn's grounds.

"I'm calling Ben right now," said Alice, digging her phone out of her bag.

When Ben picked up, Alice told him everything they'd just learned about Steve Sander. How Norman had heard him fight with Alexandra, how he'd called her by her med-school nickname, and how he'd lied about when he'd been at the inn the night of her murder. Alice stopped in her tracks as she listened to Ben's response.

"What is it?" Owen whispered. "What's he saying?"

Alice put a finger up.

"It must be a big deal," said Franny, looking at Alice worriedly. "She looks like she just saw a ghost."

CHAPTER 17

"Olivia didn't do it," said Alice, clicking off her phone and dropping it into her bag.

"So, it wasn't just the pizza!" said Franny, elbowing Owen.

"Nope. Your gut was apparently right on the money," said Owen.

"What did Ben say?" asked Franny.

"He said that Olivia *did* write that threatening letter—and that she confessed to leaving the comments on Alexandra's blog. She was furious that Alexandra had been so callous about the death of her grandmother and had always felt that there'd been an oversight in the ER that led to her death. She wanted to confront Alexandra, so she followed her here this weekend. But, Olivia couldn't have killed Alexandra, because she was at the late-night campfire at Cozy Bear. Ten people saw her there!"

"So, Norman didn't do it. Olivia didn't do it. And, we know Luke didn't do it . . ." said Owen. "Dr. Steve, come on down!"

"Did someone call me?" Steve Sander pulled up beside them in a tiny car.

"Ooh, that must be one of those electric cars," said Owen, swallowing hard. "It doesn't make a sound, does it? How very charming."

"It's cute!" said Franny, smiling awkwardly. "So tiny . . . And stealthy."

Alice's heart went into her throat. She couldn't tell how much Steve had heard of what they'd been saying, but the best thing to do was to follow Owen and Franny's lead and act like nothing was amiss.

"Um, Franny, could you text Ben and tell him to meet us? You know, for the fireworks?" Alice gave Franny a wide-eyed look.

"Sure," said Franny, taking out her phone.

"I was just telling my friends here about you," Alice said, giving Steve a friendly smile. "How you said you'd come to the bookshop. Are you still planning to stop by?"

"Sure, hop in. I'll give you a ride," he answered, returning the smile.

Alice felt a wave of relief. He must not have heard too much.

"I would, but I have my bike and all. I'll ride over and meet you there."

"It's a date!" said Steve. "I left my wallet back at the inn. I'll just run get it and see you in a bit."

Alice nodded, inadvertently glancing down at the grill of the car. That was when she saw the blood. At least that's what it looked like. Just a small smear, as though someone had tried to wipe it clean, but had missed a spot. Steve's eyes followed Alice's, and when she looked back at him, there was uneasiness there. Alice quickly recovered her composure.

"Maybe after that we can get some coffee at Joe's!" she said. "Franny makes the best coffee in town."

Steve's expression softened. "That sounds wonderful. I'll see you in a few." He turned the little car around and went back toward the inn.

"I guess he hadn't gone into town after all. That was close!" gasped Alice.

"Those electric cars make zero noise," said Owen. "We almost put our foot in it, big time."

"Thank heaven he didn't hear us," said Franny.

"Is Ben on the way?" asked Alice.

"Yes," said Franny.

"Maybe we should text him again. Tell him to—"

Suddenly, they heard the sound of gravel flying and too late, the sound of the electric car whirring upon them.

"Alice! Watch out!"

Alice heard Owen's voice and turned just in time to see the glare of the car's windshield, and the enraged face of Steve Sander behind the wheel.

CHAPTER 18

Alice had never been more grateful to live in a small town than she was that afternoon, because it only took two minutes for Owen to run back to the Valley Inn, get Samuel's old car, and return—and another two minutes for Franny and Alice to get into the car and drive the short distance to the Blue Valley ER.

Dr. Steve had driven straight for Alice in his tiny electric car, but thanks to Owen yelling, she'd jumped out of the way in the nick of time. Unfortunately, she'd fallen onto her left arm, which was now swelling up and going numb.

Doc Howard took a set of x-rays, pronounced the arm broken, and put it into a cast, ordering Alice to take it easy and wear a sling for the next six weeks.

Meanwhile, Ben had quickly apprehended Dr. Steve when his electric car had run out of juice and he'd coasted to a stop about a block from the inn. Apparently, the little vehicle could only manage to run people down a couple of times on one charge.

"Why did he kill Alexandra?" Alice asked that evening, as the group of friends sat on blankets in Luke's yard, waiting for the fireworks to get underway.

"He gave us his whole sad story after we got him behind bars," said Ben. "Seems back in medical school, Alexandra and Steve had tried to cheat on an important exam. They'd made a deal between them that if caught, they'd vouch for one another. Anyway, when rumors flew that they'd cheated, Steve kept his end of the deal, and defended himself and Alexandra before the board."

"Let me guess," said Alice. "When it was Alexandra's turn to tell her side of the story, she threw Steve under the bus."

"Yep." Ben nodded. "She even showed them evidence that Steve had cheated and managed to get off scot-free herself. After graduation, she landed in a prestigious hospital. Steve, on the other hand, was barely even allowed to finish the program, and although he did graduate and become a doctor, he was set back professionally. He couldn't get the references he needed to get ahead."

"Did he come to the conference specifically to kill Alexandra?" Franny asked. "Did he read in her blog that she'd be here?"

"Apparently not," said Ben. "It was a bit of a fluke that they both came to the conference. When Steve saw Alexandra, he snapped. He'd argued with her at the Hound that night, then went back to the inn to cool off, but instead, he just became more and more enraged."

"That's what stewing will do to you," said Owen, looking at Alice.

"What will happen to Olivia?" Alice asked.

"It's against the law to send someone a threatening letter," said Luke. "But, Olivia actually only meant to confront Alexandra. She was never going to physically harm her. Olivia has been ordered to get some counseling. We think she'll be okay. And, once again, you three had excellent instincts, by the way."

"Well, thank you," said Owen, nodding graciously.

"One more thing," said Ben, glancing at Alice, who gave him a little nod. "Alice and I want to congratulate you two on your win at the pedal boat race today. Things got so crazy, we never got to tell you." Ben raised a glass of lemonade. "Here's to this year's champions!"

Owen and Franny smiled and accepted the proffered smattering of applause from Ben, Alice, and Luke. Then Ben leaned forward and gave Franny a kiss on the cheek.

"You were worthy opponents," Owen conceded. "I guess it's time the old *Maelstrom* was put out to pasture. Or—out to sea."

"Are you kidding?" said Alice.

"I can't believe you just said that!" said Ben. "Next year, the *Maelstrom* will be back and better than ever."

"That's right!" said Alice. "There's no way you're keeping that Champion's Cup for more than a year!"

"We will return with a vengeance next summer!" said Ben.

"And, we will take you down!" said Alice.

"Bring it on!" said Owen. "We'll be ready!"

"You know, I just thought of something," said Luke. "Ben, you'll still get to have the Champion's Cup on your mantle for at least part of the year. You and Franny will be Mr. and Mrs. Maguire in just a few months."

They all paused.

"He's right," said Alice, looking at Franny, a mix of joy and sadness in her eyes. "I guess you'll be living out here on the lake pretty soon."

"Yep," said Owen, mournfully. "No more late nights in the garden together."

"What are you talking about?" Franny gave a little giggle. "I'll still be in the garden."

"You will?" Alice's smile widened. "You're still going to live above Joe's?"

Franny took Ben's hand. "Ben and I have talked about this," she said. "We love being here on the lake."

"And, we also love being over on Main Street," said Ben.

"We were trying to decide where to live—which place to give up," said Franny. "Then, we realized we don't really have to give up either place. My rent at the shop is the same whether I live in the apartment or not. So, we've decided to stay over the shop when we feel like it—and definitely when fun things are going on in town. And, we'll be out at the lake whenever we want a little more space." She smiled at Ben. "Whenever we're together, we're home. No matter where we are."

"By the way, let me remind you that Main Street is literally a five-minute bike ride from here," Ben added. "So, even when we're out here, we'll never be far."

"Two homes! I like this idea!" said Owen, clapping. "In fact, I've been thinking of getting a place out here on the lake myself someday."

"You should," said Luke. "This is a wonderful place to live." His eyes moved to Alice.

"This calls for cake!" said Owen.

"More wedding cake?" asked Franny. "Owen, I'm starting to think you're never going to be satisfied with any of them."

"Ladies and gentlemen, feast your eyes on these." Owen opened a Sourdough bakery box.

Inside were five miniature cakes, each one completely covered in brightly colored sprinkles.

"Oh," Franny breathed. "They're beautiful."

Owen passed the box around. Alice bit into her cake and smiled at the rainbow of colors that flooded the inside.

"This is a marshmallow cocoa cream cake with a creamy coffee-flavored frosting," said Owen proudly.

"It looks like Franny," said Ben, marveling at the exquisite little cake in his hand.

"It tastes like heaven," said Alice. "Every flavor in this is you, Franny."

Franny, with tears in her eyes, lunged at Owen, almost knocking him over, and hugged him. "This is my cake, Owen!"

Owen laughed and took a bite. "Yep. This is it," he said.

Alice breathed a sigh of relief and laid back on the blanket she was sharing with Luke just as the first of the fireworks boomed overhead. Luke laid down beside her, his arm behind his head, but after a moment, he rolled onto his side and laid a gentle hand on Alice's cast. "I don't ever want you in harm's way like that again," he said. "When Franny called from the hospital, before she told me you'd broken your arm, there was a moment there when I—"

"I'm fine," said Alice, putting a soothing hand on top of his.

Luke looked at her arm in its sling, then back into Alice's eyes. "The thought of losing you? Well . . . That was awful," he said. "I realized something."

A particularly spectacular firework lit up the sky, and Alice smiled up at it.

"What did you realize?" she said, looking back at Luke.

"That I—"

Finn picked that moment to walk over, give a little whimper, and insert himself between Alice and Luke. He made two small puppy circles and settled down onto the blanket, his head resting on Alice's right leg.

"Poor Finn," Alice said, petting him with her good arm. "He's probably nervous about the fireworks."

"Well, he's seriously cramping my style," said Luke, laughing and laying back down, petting Finn as well.

They admired the show for a few moments more, then Alice said, "What did you realize?"

"That I love you," said Luke quietly.

"You do?" Alice felt her heart swell.

"Yep."

"I love you, too."

"You do?"

"Yep."

"The minute this dog moves out of the way, I'm going to kiss you," Luke said, and Alice could hear the smile in his voice.

"I'll be looking forward to that," she said, feeling their hands touch on Finn's silky hair.

Alice could hear distant oooh's and ahhh's from up and down the lake—from the town dock, where the carnival lights were still flickering away, across to the

Cozy Bear, where campfires had been lit, and all the way down to Luke's cabin, where Alice lay, surrounded by the people she loved the most in the world.

She loved knowing that somewhere along the water's edge, her parents were watching the show, wrapped in their favorite old blanket. Pearl Ann and Norman were probably sitting in lawn chairs, holding hands. The Blakes, who usually brought boxes of candy over from Sugar Buzz, were passing goodies around to friends. Doc and Mrs. Howard—whose attic was now free and clear of squirrels—were somewhere out there, along with all the other townsfolk who were more like family than friends to Alice.

Luke Evans loved her, and she loved him. In that moment, all was exactly right with the world. Alice knew that tomorrow, there would be books to sell and weddings to plan—that someday, there might even be another mystery to solve.

But for now, Alice closed her eyes, feeling a warm wave of peace and gratitude, and whispered, "Thanks."

AUTHOR'S NOTE

I'd love to hear your thoughts on my books, the storylines, and anything else that you'd like to comment on —reader feedback is very important to me. My contact information, along with some other helpful links, is listed on the next page. If you'd like to be on my list of "folks to contact" with updates, release and sales notifications, etc.… just shoot me an email and let me know. Thanks for reading!

Also…

… if you're looking for more great reads, Summer Prescott Books publishes several popular series by outstanding Cozy Mystery authors.

CONTACT SUMMER PRESCOTT BOOKS PUBLISHING

Twitter: @summerprescott1

Bookbub: https://www.bookbub.com/authors/summer-prescott

Blog and Book Catalog: http://summerprescottbooks.com

Email: summer.prescott.cozies@gmail.com

YouTube: https://www.youtube.com/channel/UCngKNUkDdWuQ5k7-Vkfrp6A

And…be sure to check out the **Summer Prescott Cozy Mysteries** fan page and **Summer Prescott Books Publishing** Page on Facebook – let's be friends!

CONTACT SUMMER PRESCOTT BOOKS PUBLISHING

To download a free book, and sign up for our fun and exciting newsletter, which will give you opportunities to win prizes and swag, enter contests, and be the first to know about New Releases, click here: http://summerprescottbooks.com

Printed in Great Britain
by Amazon